I0628805

WYNDHAM SMITH

Borgo Press Books by S. Fowler Wright

Arresting Delia: An Inspector Cleveland Classic Crime Novel
The Attic Murder: An Inspector Combridge & Mr. Jellipot Classic Crime Novel
The Bell Street Murders: An Inspector Combridge & Mr. Jellipot Classic Crime Novel
Beyond the Rim: A Lost Race Fantasy
Black Widow: A Classic Crime Novel
The Blue Room: A Novel of an Alternate Future
The British Colonies: No Surrender to Nazi Germany!
The Capone Caper: Mr. Jellipot vs. the King of Crime: A Classic Crime Novel
Crime & Co.: An Inspector Cleveland Classic Crime Novel
Dawn: A Novel of Global Warming
Dead by Saturday: An Inspector Cleveland Classic Crime Novel
Dream; or, The Simian Maid: A Fantasy of Prehistory (Marguerite Cranleigh #1)
Elfwin: An Historical Novel of Anglo-Saxon Times
The End of the Mildew Gang: An Inspector Cauldron Classic Crime Novel (Mildew #3)
Four Callers in Razor Street: An Inspector Combridge & Mr. Jellipot Classic Crime Novel
Four Days' War: The Alternate World War II, Book Two
The Hanging of Constance Hillier: An Inspector Cleveland Classic Crime Novel
The Hidden Tribe: A Lost Race Fantasy
The Jordans Murder: An Inspector Combridge & Mr. Jellipot Classic Crime Novel
The King Against Anne Bickerton: A Classic Crime Novel
Megiddo's Ridge: The Alternate World War II, Book Three
The Mildew Gang: An Inspector Cauldron Classic Crime Novel (Mildew #1)
Murder in Bethnal Square: An Inspector Combridge & Mr. Jellipot Classic Crime Novel
The Police and the Public: Some Thoughts on the British System of Justice
Post-Mortem Evidence: An Inspector Combridge & Mr. Jellipot Classic Crime Novel
Prelude in Prague: The Alternate World War II, Book One
Red Ike: A Novel of Cumberland (with J. M. Denwood)
The Return of the Mildew Gang: An Inspector Cauldron Classic Crime Novel (Mildew #2)
The Rissole Mystery: An Inspector Combridge & Mr. Jellipot Classic Crime Novel
The Screaming Lake: A Lost Race Fantasy
The Secret of the Screen: An Inspector Combridge & Mr. Jellipot Classic Crime Novel
The Song of Songs and Other Poems
Spiders' War: A Novel of the Far Future (Marguerite Cranleigh #3)
Three Witnesses: A Classic Crime Novel
Too Much for Mr. Jellipot: An Inspector Combridge & Mr. Jellipot Classic Crime Novel
The Vengeance of Gwa: A Fantasy of Prehistory (Marguerite Cranleigh #2)
Was Murder Done? A Classic Crime Novel
Who Murdered Reynard? A Classic Crime Novel
The Wills of Jane Kanwhistle: An Inspector Combridge & Mr. Jellipot Classic Crime Novel
With Cause Enough?: An Inspector Combridge & Mr. Jellipot Classic Crime Novel
Wyndham Smith: His Adventures in the 45th Century: A Science Fiction Novel

WYNDHAM SMITH

HIS ADVENTURES IN THE 45TH CENTURY

A Science Fiction Novel

by

S. FOWLER WRIGHT

THE BORGO PRESS

An Imprint of Wildside Press LLC

MMIX

Copyright © 1938 by S. Fowler Wright
Copyright © 2009 by the Estate of S. Fowler Wright

Originally published as *The Adventure of Wyndham Smith.*

All rights reserved.
No part of this book may be reproduced in any form
without the expressed written consent
of the author and publisher.

www.wildsidebooks.com

FIRST WILDSIDE EDITION

CHAPTER ONE

Wyndham Smith was at Guy's Hospital at the time he had his experience, a medical student in his second year.

He looked round a room floored and walled and furnished in the same substance, which was strange to him— "ebonied glass" came to his mind—and across at a man who was strangely dresses—Oriental?—no, not exactly that—and with an aspect of age with in the grave dignity of his face, and of youth in the smooth freshness of his skin, who was saying in a distant and yet not unfriendly way: "I suppose you are puzzled as to where you have come?"

"Once before," he replied, "I had a dream something like this. I mean, I knew I was dreaming the while I dreamed. I remember hoping I should not wake till the end came; but this is the most vivid dream that I even had."

The man's lips moved to a slight smile. "You need have no fear about that."

"No? I feel as though I were awake now."

"So you are."

Wyndham Smith looked round. He considered the polished shadows of the walls, and the brighter opaqueness of the ceiling which gave a diffused light to the room. He was not convinced.

"Then, perhaps," he said, "You will explain how I got here."

It was a reasonable request, though he saw that a dream might invent an answer of no reliable value.

"That," the protagonist of his dream replied, "is what I propose to do. It is a courtesy which I might have extended freely to a young man of your profession, but it is necessary apart from that. It is important here from the early part of the twentieth century. You are now—by an extension of your system of reckoning—in the later part of the forty-fifth."

"You can't expect me to swallow that."

"No? I wonder why. Has the idea of such transmigration, either voluntary or enforced, never entered your mind? Even so, you have had some years of training which should make you receptive to new ideas. I thought that yours was a time when the implications of relativity began to be understood."

"I am afraid," Wyndham Smith said honestly, "that I am one of those to whom the implications of relativity are not clear. I am willing to believe that time is the fourth dimension which has a plausible sound. But I don't go far beyond that. As to people being able to jump about in time, from one age to another, even if it were shown in theory that they could—which would be hard to believe— observation tells us definitely that it doesn't occur."

"May I ask how you have been able to observe that?"

"If it did, people would appear suddenly among us from nowhere, and others would disappear in the same way. You couldn't even take a census."

"You are half right and half wrong. Your year was nineteen thirty-seven, was it not, in the reckoning of your day?"

"Yes, that's what it is now."

"Ye-es. No man has gone back to that period, or is likely to do so. Having known it, you can't be surprised. But they have been fetched away in large numbers, English people in your century being a favourite selection for many purposes. I learned your language from one of them."

"I know that isn't true. If it were, we should notice they had disappeared."

The older man was unmoved by the bluntness of this contradiction. "If you think," he said, with a quiet certainty, "you will know that it is…did you never hear of the number of people who disappeared in England at that time—even in London alone—every month? What do you suppose had become of them?"

"I suppose that they had changed their names, or wandered away."

"Do you know the proportion of them that were never found?"

"Not exactly. I know it was a large number."

Wyndham Smith remembered reading a newspaper account of such disappearances a few days before. (Was it that which had given him this most vivid dream?) He could not recall the figures, but he knew that the number who were never traced had been described as very large— "inexplicably large" had been the expression used. He was frank about that, both to himself and the stranger to whom he spoke. He added, "But, at most, that doesn't prove that they disappeared into futurity: it only fails to disprove that anyone did."

"Yes. But, at least, it proves that you were wrong in the reason you gave for discrediting such a possibility."

"I must admit that," he answered with the same frankness as before, and with a growing disposition not to contest the possibility further. After all, why not let a dream have its way?

The stranger seemed to perceive without further words that it was accepted as a hypothesis on which the conversation could be continued. He went on: "It is necessary that you should be informed as to where you are, owing to the experience which is before you, the nature of which will naturally be grasped more readily by one who has had some training in medical science, however elementary, than it would be by most others of the period from which you come.

"It was partially understood in your own time, though the idea itself was less clearly perceived than were its implications and consequences, that the individual man is of dual personality. The seat of the ego—the man himself, as distinguished from the physical body which had been formed from ancestral cell—was vaguely located in the hinder part of the brain, and that location has since been more exactly fixed.

"With the advance of surgery, the grafting or exchange of the major organs of the body naturally led to the consideration of the possibility that the ego itself might be transferred. But that which was simple in theory was found to be difficult in practice, owing to the fact that the cell—if that word be allowed—of which the ego consists was found to be so small that its minuteness is beyond human comprehension, if not measurement; and that, for the operation to be successfully performed, it must be transferred without the remotest trace of surrounding matter,"

"I remember," Wyndham remarked, accepting the initial improbability to which he had been introduced in his interest in this explanation, "in…in my own time that an American scientist calculated that if the germs from which every Englishman had originated since the Norman conquest were heaped together, they would never cover a needle's point."

"That," the stranger answered, after a moment's pause, "must have been, by an extremely large margin, within the truth; but the germ-cells of which you speak are themselves as much larger than the essential ego as the space occupied by our planetary system exceeds the size of its central sun."

"But you say that these difficulties have been overcome?" Wyndham asked.

Since he had decided to abandon himself without resistance to the course of this vivid dream, the quiet authority and assurance of the stranger's words were bringing conviction to a mind which had been trained to learn and accept surprising facts from the lecturers of his own profession. He had a vague but pleasing vision of himself as being sent back to his own time by this courteous and able stranger after learning such things as would place him in the forefront of the scientists of his time.

Was it—his mind wandered to ask—by this method that the great "discoveries" of past generations had been communicated to those who had given them to the world, without revealing a source of knowledge which would have discounted their own eminence, if it had not been received with derision, or introduced them to a sorcerer's stake? Was it such an experience that had come to the friend of Paul when, in his own words, "he was caught up to the third heaven, and heard unspeakable things"?

"They have been overcome," the stranger replied, "but not easily. The operation requires elaborate preparations, and can only be performed at long intervals, and upon not more than four individuals—that is two exchanges—at once."

"May I ask what is the result of the operation, if every trace of surrounding matter should not be successfully separated?"

"Insanity—at the least. Insanity both to the ego transferred with adhesions which will be foreign to the brain with which new relations must be established, and to that which is introduced to a depleted environment."

"And if it be successful? I suppose that the knowledge—the memories—"

"You suppose rightly. I see that you perceive some of the limitations of the results of this operation, and the possibilities that remain."

"I should have thought—"

"Yes. You would have guessed correctly, so far as guessing would be likely to go; and beyond that you would have seen that only experiment could resolve the enigmas your mind would raise. But the time for guessing is past.

"If you will listen carefully, on a matter which is likely to be of the utmost interest to yourself, it is what I propose to explain."

Wyndham did not like that expression "of the utmost interest to yourself." He did not like the way it was said. His heart missed a beat. Was he to be the subject of one of these interesting experiments?

The thought was one from which he shrank in a most unscientific spirit. The beauties of vivisection—even its moral altitudes are matters which the vivisected may fail to see. He was glad to recall—which he had been so near to forget—that you cannot die, nor suffer hurt, in a dream. He made no answer; and the stranger, after a moment of keen though quiet scrutiny, as though reading his mind very easily, commenced the explanation he had promised to give.

"I should tell you first that it has been practicable, for a very long period, to transfer all parts of the principal organs of the body, so that the anomaly was no longer possible (for instance) by which a scientist might be frustrated in his work by a defective gall bladder or a sluggish liver, while a common lunatic would be going about with these organs robustly alive. Grafting or substitution would quickly restore the physical harmony which the quality of his work required.

"You will not suppose that such results were achieved without some unexpected difficulties, some unforeseen complications, some inevitable catastrophes. But the practice is now firmly established, and it might be difficult to find a man of more than eighty or a hundred years, one or more of whose vital organs have not been substantially or radically repaired.

"You will see that this custom had beneficent consequences in ameliorating the conditions of the poor, for no child could be born who was not potentially valuable, if not in itself, yet to prolong the existence of others; and to the meanest of mankind there was opened the high, unselfish destiny that his lungs might expand with a monarch's breath, or his heart beat in a statesman's breast.

"For those wretched females who were allowed to marry, before the era of the present orderly methods, there was the hope that, if they could produce offspring of more than average quality, and with the requisite regularity, their lives might be indefinitely prolonged by a grateful country; and there were some whose bodies were so successfully repaired or renewed that they lived for more than two hundred years.

"Nor must you suppose that the direct benefits of this advance in surgical science were confined to those who were eminent in the state, or required for the continuance of its population. Purchases and exchanges became frequent among all classes of the community, and no cause of litigation was more common than that arising from this description of bartering. A man complaining, for instance, that he had been led by fraudulent misrepresentation to surrender a sound stomach for a heart with a defective valve. And as you will easily see, that at least three persons, and probably more, must have been directly involved in each of these transactions, for a few men would desire to make a direct exchange of the same organ only, and none would wish to be left with two of the same kind. The equitable adjustment of these disputes might be far from simple, and the cancellation of the contract by the return to a man of his own property might be unfair to an innocent party not directly concerned in the dispute."

"It is an idea," Wyndham took advantage of a moment's pause to remark, forgetting his previous fear in the interest of the subject, "of many fascinating possibilities, but I should suppose that, in such cases as the women you mentioned, whose ages must have been over two hundred, there could be so little of the originals left that the question of identity would arise. Would they not have ceased to be the persons that they first were, and become compilations of other and younger women?"

"It is a question which naturally and necessarily arose at a comparatively early time, when major operations of this kind were first recognized as being of a beneficent and practicable character. It was a line of defence in an ancient and famous trial, when a wealthy criminal distributed his vital organs so freely among his associates (even including some portions of the brain itself) that there arose a serious issue of how far the human form in the dock could be held responsible for the deeds with which it was charged, or how otherwise the criminal could be brought to justice.

"The case actually resulted in an acquittal, it being decided that the man had escaped beyond the possibility of arrest, and it was this trial which led the government of that day to set aside a large fund for the determination of the location of personality in the human body...with an ultimate consequence which has brought you here."

The last remark was a sharp reminder to Wyndham Smith that his interest in the instruction he was receiving might not prove to be of a merely academic kind. And feeling, like the man about to be hanged, that he could bear anything but suspense, he put the question directly, "And do you mind telling me what that is?"

"It is to that that I was about to come. But, before giving you such information, I wish you to have a clear mind as to the nature and consequence of the transfer of the human ego from one body to another.

"In the first place, our experiments have demonstrated that the ego has an identity absolutely separate from the body which it inhabits, and over which it has a limited muscular control. It follows, as you may have anticipated, that when an ego is transferred, it leaves behind all the memories, all the knowledge, which were stored in the brain which it had previously governed, and acquires the knowledge and memories of the one which it commences to occupy.

"It might be supposed that the practical result would be as though there had been no transfer at all. But this is not so. The ego which enters the body of another inherits the knowledge which that brain has acquired, and the physical dexterities to which it has trained its members, but does not necessarily sympathize with the proclivities which have caused that knowledge to be accumulated, or those physical abilities to develop; it may commence at once to train its acquired brain to other uses, its body to different sports.

"Having explained this, you will understand that if (for instance) your own ego should be removed from your present body and another introduced, the fresh tenant would acquire memory of this conversation, and would therefore readily understand what had occurred on an explanation being supplied. And, in the same way, if you should be transferred to another body, you would be equally so informed if the knowledge had been previously so imparted to the brain of which you would obtain control."

"You mean," Wyndham replied, endeavouring to maintain an impersonal attitude towards the subject, and suppressing the cold fear of a more immediate interest, "that if (for instance) my ego were so transferred, I should lose the memories that I now have, with all the knowledge of the time from which you say that I am already so widely removed, and should be dependent upon you to inform me even of the fact of my present identity?"

"That is what the position would be, but, in place of all from which you would have parted, you would have acquired the use of the stores of another brain, and its natural abilities, which might be more—perhaps much more—than those you had left behind, and of which also—it is an equal chance—you might make more energetic and successful use than had the ego by which they were previously controlled."

"That is quite clear," Wyndham admitted; "and I can recognize it as logical probability, though it is less easy to accept as a possible eventuality; but may I ask"—and he could not entirely control his voice, as he said this, to the casual tone which he desired to use—"why you should be giving me this information? May I, perhaps, be privileged to watch such an experiment, so that I may describe it when I—" He was near to saying "When I wake: up," but substituted "When I return to my own time," as being more courteous to his auditor. For the denizens of a dream cannot desire to be made conscious of their own unsubstantiality, of which even the dreamer may not be aware while the dream endures. But was it really a dream?—if he could only be a little surer of that!

If—it was the next moment's thought—if he could only awake! For the answer to which he was listening confirmed the worst of his secret dread: "You have—as I can see that you are sufficiently intelligent to anticipate—the exceptional honour of having been chosen from among millions of your time and race to be the subject of such an experiment."

Wyndham Smith did not respond with an aspect of gratitude to this complimentary assurance. He strove to convince himself that the danger which appeared to threaten him was too remote from reality—too fantastic to fear. Yet if—indeed—

"May I ask whether, if I should submit to so strange an experience, I may ultimately be restored to my own identity?"

"I regret that I cannot reply to that question, for the answer, even if I know it, which you need not assume, will give information to the ego which will shortly control your body, which it might not be convenient for it to have. For the moment I must leave you, there being no more to say."

As he spoke, the stranger rose from his seat and passed out through the solid-seeming wall, which gave way before him as having no substance whatever.

Wyndham Smith was left alone to consider the fate to which he was incredibly destined. It was a suggestion of fantastic horror, and yet—he remembered a remark which had been made by Professor Kortright at the lecture last Tuesday night. He had explained, as a surprising fact, that a man has no regard for the welfare of the corpuscles, even for the nerves of his own body, so long as he does not share their danger, or while they are powerless to hurt him with any message of their own pain.

He had said that the benefits which had resulted, in certain classes of operations, from the use of local, in addition to general anaesthetics, demonstrated that the general one does not prevent the torture of the isolated nerves, but only frustrates their efforts to awaken those of the brain itself to a kindred anguish.

Yet how many, he asked, would pay an extra fifty pounds, or even ten, to save the nerves of his own limb from such an experience, if assured that he himself would be unable to feel the pain? They would be roused to readier sympathy by some tale of the abuse of a dog in a distant town!

"I myself"—those had been the professor's words, and in saying them had he not implied all the distinction between the ego and the inhabited body which had been the theme of their discourse of the previous half-hour?

With this thought, there came also the supposition that that lecture might have supplied the idea from which this dream was born. Surely that must be so, and—unutterable relief. It was no more than a dream—indeed, a dream therefore from which it must be possible to wake, and that waking Wyndham resolved that he would no longer delay. Not but that it might have been of interest to penetrate somewhat farther into the fantasy that the dream proposed—if only, while he did so, he could be sure that it were no more.

But the uncertainty was too great to be longer endured. He was resolved to wake from a nightmare which was become too real. And then he found that it was something he could not do. Surely you could wake from a dream? Surely, surely, when you strove to wake with your utmost will, with the whole mind concentrated on what must be the waking vision—the window opposite, which must be visible in the moonlit night (Wyndham remembered that there was a moon that was near the full), the bed-rail, the familiar walls...

But the familiar walls did not return. He saw only the ebonised, glassy surface through which the stranger had so absurdly, so impossibly, passed away. He would resolve for himself if it were substance or shadow that held him now. He rose and walked to the wall.

He felt a substance that was neither cold nor warm, being of the same temperature as the hand that he pressed against it. But otherwise it was polished granite to feel: granite-hard, granite-smooth. He paused at the place where his late companion had vanished, feeling it with patience and care. But it was all equally smooth, equally hard. Very surely it was a dream. But it was a dream that he could not break.

CHAPTER TWO

And now Wyndham Smith—if it were he, if he can be properly identified in that lithe, exotic figure in the single garment of purple, so different from the appearance of the medical student that he had been a few hours (or was it something more than two millenniums?) before—stretched himself on a bed. The hour must have been near to noon, for the sun shone downward into the roofless chamber from a blue cloud-flecked sky, but he was conscious of nothing strange in being stretched supine at the highest hour of the day.

He lay busy enough, for he was occupied with his own thoughts, and it was the only occupation that most men had in the only world that he now knew. For he knew nothing now of the experiences of the body which he had once controlled, to which its parents had given the title of Wyndham Smith.

Colpeck-4XP lay on the bed, remembering that he had agreed only yesterday that his ego should be transferred to that of a primitive of the commencement of the machine age, whose ego should have control of his own body for—it had not been clear for how long. Then he could not be Colpeck-4XP? He must, in reality, be Wyndham Smith. It was no use to resent that, as he oddly did. He was himself, and should be satisfied with his conscious life, and the control of so perfect and important a physical personality. If it were true that he had once inhabited the body of a primitive, half-witted savage of the early machine age, how unbelievably fortunate he now was!

Yet, queerly, all the force of a powerful intellect found itself in difficulty when it strove to persuade him thus. All the bodily consciousness which was not his own ego, but which had subserved another for many years, rose up in impatient protest against the alien control that it now felt, and, because his own consciousness worked through it, its resentment was not easy to thrust away.

Yet it must be done. He was aware, for it was a remembered conversation of yesterday, that the ego which would waken today in the body of Colpeck-4XP was to be that of the primitive, Wyndham Smith, and that the intention had been to discover how one of that early age would react to the traditions and environment that he would inherit with his new body—and to the world crisis which was to culminate before the end of the present day. A foolish, futile thing, for the event was agreed, and he had given his own ready assent. It was worthwhile, if only because it was an adventure of a kind, after the possibilities of adventure had long been lost to the hopes or fears of an ordered world.

He had agreed only yesterday about that, though perhaps with somewhat less alacrity than some others, for life was not entirely unpleasant, even in these terrible days—but he had agreed. At least—he?—or was it another who had assented then? He remembered the promise he had made yesterday afternoon that when he waked today he would review the whole question with a firm resolution to put aside all previous bias or decision, and face the sombre prospect anew. Well, he would do that fairly enough, useless as he knew it to be. For he would weigh that which was no less than a settled and certain thing. How far back should he now begin?

Perhaps it would be best to go back even to the very beginning of civilizations to the utter barbarism of the period from which he supposed that he himself had come. The time which had half-emerged from the primitive custom of manual labour, and had self-styled itself the Machine Age, having no imagination of the end of that far road on which it had taken the first blind, blundering steps.

Then they had made their crude machines with their own hardened, discoloured hands. They had not even realized, in a denseness difficult to comprehend, that the stored energies of the earth could be so utilized and controlled that they would do the work of men without help beyond that of the human brain—that machines would make each other far better than they had first been erected by human hands. With a comic futility, they had sat in the machines they made, moving, to no useful end, about the surface of the earth, while their machines collided continually, killing both those who were seated therein, and those who walked in the same ways—killing and maiming to a total that rose into millions of ended or damaged lives— and still they who remained would climb into their machines, and start them whirling about to increase the tale of the dead.

A wild, incredible age. An age of nations and wars. Perhaps it was hardly necessary to go back so far. There were so many things that existed then which had ceased to be. So many conditions of life that were now no more than an evil, alluring dream. After that, there had been the abolition of war. The abolition of nationality. The abolition of social inequalities. The abolition of the barbarisms of competition. The control or abolition of every form of animal or insect life. The control of climate, with the consequent abolition of extremes of temperature or discomforts of tempest. The almost absolute abolition of disease. Finally, the abolition of pain, complete and final, as evidenced by the fact that he felt no smallest discomfort from the operation which must have been performed upon him.

So mankind had risen and proved its strength, coming to a serene supremacy over the follies and failures of earlier millenniums, and over the physical forces to which they had once succumbed. And so, at last, for five hundred years, they had endured a life which was without difference or result, without hope or fear, except the fear of its individual end, which would now approach, at a steady pace, to a settled date, until now, to break the monotony of eventless years, a new idea had been born. It had originated in the mind of Pilwin-C6P and was no less than that the incompetence of the Creator should be challenged and demonstrated by the universal suicide of mankind.

Languidly, indifferently with most, but with an occasional individual eagerness or enthusiasm, it had been endorsed by the huge majority of the five million adults who were now the total population of an ordered world. It had been agreed unanimously from hundred to hundred, rising in the intellectual scale (which was now immeasurable with an exact accuracy, and had become the sole basis of political organization), until it required no more than the assent of the final hundred—which he was one—to be operated of immediately.

The mind from which the suggestion had come was one from which a new idea would be likely to emanate, if any originality of purpose should still be possible to the human brain. It was not merely that he had himself the eminence of being in the first hundred. The Pilwins, for nearly two thousand years, had been intellectually distinguished, and over sixty percent of the seven hundred who now bore that name were among the first million in the mental ranking of mankind—a percentage with which even the Colpecks could not compare.

Besides that, the name had a conspicuous record for individual initiatives in earlier centuries. It was a Pilwin who had removed the ice-caps of the poles. It was another Pilwin who had conceived the bold, successful project (already partly accomplished) of destroying all forms of alien life, in one comprehensive motion, by spreading a concrete-like substance over the major portions of the earth's surface, reserving only such limited areas as might still be required for the production of human food. Not that this was an invention of any Pilwin brain. Even in barbarous times many small portions of the earth's surface had been spread with concrete, so that all possibilities of life had ceased, both beneath or above it. But that had been done without deliberate intention: a mere careless gesture of blasphemy against the Creator of life. It was a Pilwin who had first conceived it as a means of sterilising the earth in a widespread way.

It was the same Pilwin who had proposed a chemical process which would have sterilised the oceans also, though that had been obstructed by fear of sinister incidental consequences which only the experiment could have resolved; and it was another who had formulated the orderly and convenient method by which the generations were kept twenty-five years apart.

Considering the brilliant achievements of the Pilwin intellect, Wyndham Smith (as we may still conveniently call him, though with a somewhat dubious accuracy, as he reviews Colpeck's memories in a Colpeck's brain) observed that it was this custom of the quarter-century intervals that rendered the proposal of Pilwin-C6P so particularly opportune, since it meant that there were no children to be consulted, or consigned to possibly reluctant end: for a child might still exist for a space of years before the love of life would be wholly gone.

Wyndham Smith, reviewing the various arguments in favour of this procedure which his brain had evolved or heard during the last two months, and pleasantly conscious of intellectual freedom and audacity such as his ego had not previously experienced, was obliged, though with some amount of irrational reluctance, to make frank acknowledgment of their weight and quality.

The work of mankind might have been worth the doing, or it might not. But be that as it might, it was at least clear that that work was done. Man had come to complete supremacy over the earth, and—greater difficulty—over himself also. Contending forms of life had been eliminated or suppressed. The major physical forces of the planet, which had made him their early sport, were now in harness. The discords and confusions which had set nation against nation, class against class, were no more than traditions of muddled incompetence, becoming increasingly difficult to realize, if not to believe.

Every form of struggle or competition, every variety of hardship, disease, or pain, had been eliminated—and was it possible to regret that? If there be competition, there must be those who will fall behind. Victory must involve defeat, which is a barbarously unpleasant experience. If, as the result, they had merely discovered that, if there be none behind, there can be none in front, that pleasure ends with the cessation of pain, was it a responsibility which could be laid at any other than the Creator's door?

Now, with nothing left either to hope or fear, the generations would come and go. Every twenty-five years a quantity of selected children would be added to the population of the world. In the same period, the same number of people would pass into painless death. A generation would be born, and another die. But what use was there in that? A futile, aimless, endless monotony, which—wonderful, single remaining power—it yet lay in their hands to bring to a seemly close. Yes—the arguments were not easy to overset.

And this evening, at the eighteenth hour, the First Hundred were to meet to adopt or discard the proposal which had first come from themselves, and had since been agreed with unanimity by the whole remaining population of the world. And it was understood that it would be agreed tonight with the same unanimity—probably without discussion—unless he only were to resist.

It was only because the First Hundred would exhaust every possibility of preventing error on so momentous an issue, even when there was no doubt or division among themselves, that they had introduced him, an alien ego, to one of their own best brains, to observe how he would react to its accumulated knowledge, its recollected experiences, its instinctive emotions.

He—and he only—would be liable to resist the decision of a united world, and though he was still resolved to consider the problem in every aspect as the sun declined through the long hours of the afternoon, it was a resistance that he had little inclination to offer. Should not the curtain make its orderly fall at the close of an ended play?

CHAPTER THREE

Wyndham Smith looked around the spacious, low-ceilinged room which he knew so well. In its midst was a table, long and large, around which were a hundred seats. His acquaintance of the previous night sat at the head, and his own seat was third away on the left.

He looked at that which he scarcely saw, for his mind was occupied with the question which brought him there, and his eyes encountered familiar things. Had he still occupied the body in which he came, he would have been intrigued and puzzled by many strange and some inexplicable experiences which had been his since he had left his own room less than an hour before, but which he had not regarded at all, as he would have been baffled by the sounds of a strange tongue. For the language which he now heard was not that in which Wyndham Smith had been first addressed, which had been that of his own tongue and his own time.

He would have been puzzled even by such details as that he was not aware of any freshness or staleness of air, which was alike in an unroofed space, or in the crowd of that shallow room; but, as it was, his mind could work oblivious of surrounding sights, and only negatively aware of the familiar faces around him now. Faces that had differences of type and colour, and yet would have seemed strangely, bafflingly, even terribly alike to the wonder of his previous eyes.

They were faces of some difference, in that they showed faint traces of various races, but they were alike in an impression of intellectual power of a passive sort, and still more so in a lack of animation, of physical character, which left them passionless and serene as death. It was, indeed, to the serenity of the newly dead, before corruption has seized its prey, that they may be most accurately compared, although it was clear enough that they possessed a vigour of physical life which was too constant for their regard.

Wyndham was aware—it was a routine fact, which did not need to be said—that, though they sat without visible audience, all that was spoken there would be heard by the five million population of the whole world, and would be decisive and final, if—as there could be little reason to doubt—it should approve the plan which had already received the support of all the lesser intellects of the human race.

The chairman, three seats away, commenced without rising, and without preamble or any form of address. His visible audience turned faces towards him which were gravely, unemotionally, attentive, and controlled even a faint tremor of excitement, not at the near prospect of their own extinction, but of the intellect only, at the thought of an event unprecedented, when it had seemed that all novelty must have left the world.

"We have met," he said, "to record our votes upon a resolution which has been adopted unanimously by those of lower intelligence, and which may have been discussed sufficiently by themselves, of which discussions we are all more or less completely aware. The resolution is that we shall release ourselves from the aimless burden of life by a general euthanasia which is to be arranged for the seventh noon after today. It is a course which, if it be adopted, must be unanimous, for if there be exceptions, however few, its central purpose will be upset, which is to rebuke the Creative Power by the complete self-ending of human life.

"Expressing no opinion myself, from which my position requires me to abstain until yours be known, I will ask each of you in turn whether the resolution has your support, that our verdict may be known to all those who hear."

Having said this, he addressed those who sat round the table, one by one, calling them by their distinctive numerals, and by the names of their houses, "Do you agree or dissent?" And the replies came in a steady, toneless monotony, "I agree..." "I agree..."—only the voices of the women, who were about equally numerous, being slightly softer than those of the men.

It was indeed by their voices that an alien onlooker would most readily have decided which were the women, for the dresses of all—a single garment of purple—were alike, and the hair of all was trimmed in the same way.

As the chairman commenced on his right, it followed that ninety-six of the hundred names had been called before it came to Wyndham's turn to reply. He sat listening to that monotonous chorus, of assents, and he was unsure, even then, what he would say when his time should come. His reason told him that the human race had served whatever purpose it had, and that there was an absurdity in continuing it perpetually through succeeding generations with the endless iteration of a recurring decimal.

This perception was not complicated by any theory of there being a permanent value in the individual life, or a survival from death, for such beliefs had long left the world. They had no place in the brain which he now controlled, and, even in that which his ego had ruled before, they had been regarded as too unsubstantial to affect the actual conduct of life. They had been rejected finally by implication fifteen hundred years later, when it had been resolved to limit the human race to five million selected lives.

In that resolution, which had sought no more than to limit births to a number which could realize (it had been supposed) the maximum comforts and pleasures of human existence, there had been the seed of that which was put forward today.

But though the new brain of Wyndham Smith might be fecund of arguments in support of the resolution, which it seemed, as the names were called, that all others approved, his ego, fresh from the strifes and discords of a different world, was still half unwilling to own their weight—would indeed have been resolved to reject them, but for a dreadful doubt which had arisen to confuse feeling and tend to enlist it in reason's cause. If he should dissent from the resolution, and it should thus founder for lack of the unanimity which it required, would he be allowed to continue in this life, which, with all its futile negation, was the only one that he now knew? Or would he be sent back to the unimaginable horrors and barbarisms from which he had been made aware, however feeling might revolt, that his ego came?

And then, diversely, against this instinctive revulsion that was clamorous in the pain-free body, his new-found intellect asked: if that life to those who lived it was less endurable than is yours today, why was not self-destruction then a more general thing? But yet—cold, misery, pain (his body had once felt pain, in his early days, and it was an experience he would not forget), perhaps hunger and thirst, perhaps even compulsory uncongenial toil—would they not change the present dreariness of existence to more active hell? And it would soon be his turn to speak, for the voices of those who answered were near him now.

He became aware that all eyes were upon him, with a stir of interest, of expectation, which had not been evident as the question had been asked and answered till now; and he understood that they must all be aware that though they looked at a familiar form, and knew that it was controlled by a Colpeck brain, they knew also that its ego was of a distant age. He was the last insurance against mistake which the chairman had thought it prudent to introduce. And it was to him that the chairman was speaking now— "Do you agree or dissent?"

He heard his voice, and seemed to learn from it for the first time what his answer would be. "I dissent."

The stir of interest, of expectation, was more pronounced. His memory told him that the assembly had not been equally moved—slight as its emotion might now be—by any previous event that it had considered within his time. But the chairman showed no emotion, no surprise, at this reply which might deny the will of almost the whole of the human race. He asked quietly, "Do you dissent from a settled mind, or do you desire that the question be more discussed?"

"I would have it further discussed."

"Then it is so it shall be."

The chairman went on with the formal questions, taking the replies of the remaining two, and when it had been heard that they also agreed, so that Wyndham Smith was the sole dissenting voice in the world of men, he turned his attention to him again, with a question which was the routine of such a position.

"By what argument do you dissent?"

Wyndham did not find it easy to answer that. He might have said that he felt an instinctive antipathy to self-destruction, that his was a fighting ego which was not willing to own defeat; but he knew that his feelings had not been asked. It was reason he was invited to give.

There was a pause of silence before he said, "It is that which should be done completely, if it be attempted at all. From most evil conditions man has struggled free at the last, and has found—as you are agreed—that there is nothing better beyond, that he has come by a hard road to a house where no treasure lies. If we are so certain of that, should we not end all life, and not only ourselves? Should we not sterilize the land and sea so that life, which, there is sound reason to think, is a peculiarity of this planet alone, will come to its final end? For else, may not life assert itself in a new form which will be akin to that which we have destroyed, and our protest be a Creator's jest?"

It was not what he intended to urge. It was merely the first criticism which could be supplied by a brain which did not respond to the feeling which called upon it. In the long minutes of silence that followed—which were no more than the customary courtesy which all speakers received at that assembly, where haste was a forgotten word, and it would have been thought unmannerly to answer without a pause of consideration—he had a better thought, which he also spoke:

"Also, if it be allowed that we have come by a bad road to no better end, there is yet a choice which we might prefer to take rather than that which is so nearly agreed. We can go back by the way we came, to find, perhaps, a somewhat different advance to a fairer goal."

His words fell into the same silence, which they prolonged. He was not surprised at that, his brain being familiar with the ways of his fellow-men. He became aware that this silence was shared by five millions beyond those walls, who had supposed few moments before, that their own voices had sealed their doom.

Pilwin-C6P was the first to speak. He said, "It could be done. It might be the better way. Nor need it long defer that on which we are already resolved."

He thought only of the first proposal that Wyndham made. Being the one who had originated the idea of the cessation of human life, he would have been likely to support the resolution with more than average decision, but

Wyndham's argument recalled the proposal his ancestor had made for the sterilization of the oceans, which had been rejected at that time for reasons which would have lost their force if it should be preceded by the extinction of human life. He saw his ancestor justified at the last; and though any feeling of pride or satisfaction in the prestige or achievements of his clan, or of an individual ancestor, would have been esteemed a barbaric indecency, such as he would not have admitted, even to himself, that he could be degraded to feel, yet the atavistic instinct stirred faintly beneath his mind, rendering him more tolerant of Wyndham's argument than he would otherwise have become.

It was a point on which he spoke with authority, and the chairman, after a pause of a few minutes to give opportunity for any further comment, and seeing that all were silent in acceptance of the statement that Pilwin-C6P had made, gave his ruling thereon.

"The first amendment," he said, "which has been proposed, is no more than a point of detail, such as may be resolved here without the delay which a general reference would require. On the assurance which we have received that the elimination of life in non-human forms could be completed without complicating the major proposition, I am prepared to rule that we may authorize that such steps be taken immediately that the resolution itself be accepted with the unanimity which it requires."

He addressed Wyndham directly as he concluded, "If you can accept the resolution on that condition being agreed, your second argument will not arise."

But Wyndham had also had time for thought. He was clear now as to his own will, and his arguments were gaining order and strength in a mind that must respond to a new control. "But," he replied, "it is the second which I prefer."

The chairman regarded him with a gravity which approached rebuke. If the removal of the first objection would leave him unsatisfied, what point had there been in considering it at all? But he saw that, by a fine distinction of logic, this objection might be repulsed. For Wyndham had allowed that he was open to argument on the main proposal, and it might be that, if he should be persuaded that his second proposition was of an impossible quality, he might then accept the resolution with the newly accepted condition attached thereto, which he would otherwise have declined.

He asked, "You propose that men should go back to the barbarism from which they came?"

"I propose that men might revert to conditions of less settled security."

Had Wyndham Smith been, in his previous body, in control of the brain it held, he would doubtless have surprised the assembly by following this statement with a speech in its support, which might have lengthened into thousands of randomly chosen words; but he knew that the custom here was of a more orderly kind.

The debate which went on for the next two hours was a matter of grave and silent consideration, frequently punctuated by brief, pregnant, carefully worded remarks, many of which were of such a nature as to give no indication of the side to which the speaker's mind was disposed to lean. The members of the assembly appeared to be too absolute in self-control, or too deficient in emotional vitality, to be stirred to any mental excitement, or emphasis of expression, by the momentous nature of the question with which they dealt. Only the ego of Wyndham Smith, accustomed to the urgencies of more strenuous days, was restrained with effort to the same outward placidity by the traditions of the brain of which he had so recently gained control.

But from the pregnant silence, these occasional observations, an opinion gradually emerged that there would be a probably insuperable difficulty in obtaining any general measure of agreement as to the extent or nature of the retrogression to be undertaken; an almost invincible reluctance to face once more the pains and dangers from which mankind had escaped by so bitter and long a way. The unanimity which had accepted its own defeat, which had agreed upon the fulfilment, if not the frustration, of human destiny, could not be anticipated even for the abstract principle of an alternative which must be repulsive to the finer instincts of every sensitive and civilized mind; and still less would there be any probability of agreement upon the details of retreat to the savageries of competition, the horrors of death and pain.

It was Pilwin-C6P, seeing the imminent prospect that the plan for which he felt parent's affection would go down before the opposition of a single man (and he, as they all knew, being no more than the ego a distant, barbarous age), who proposed the solution which would be sufficient save it.

"Why," he asked, "should it not be resolved that each man be free to follow the preference of his own heart? Let it be decreed that he who declines the high gesture of human suicide, by which mankind will reject the life which it has not asked, and has found to be no more than the gift of a jesting god, may revert to such barbarisms as a baser nature may prefer."

There was so near an approach, as he said this, to outdated passion in words and tone, and the proposition itself was so amazing—for it had been the fundamental principle of the proposed event that should extinguish human life with an entire finality—that it would have produced a clamour of bewildered protest in an assembly of a more volatile kind. As it was it was followed by a universal silence, in which the first stupefactions of surprise gave way to understanding and then consent.

For, even though this Colpeck of alien ego should elect (fantastic thought!) to remain in solitary discord when the whole procession of his fellow-men should have passed through the gates of death, it would still appear a fantasy beyond serious consideration that he should find a companion of kindred mood. Solitary as he would be—with no possibility of procreation remaining—he might plumb such depths of barbarism as his soul desired, might prolong his absurdity of existence to its latest hour, and he would be no more than a final mockery in his Creator's eyes, an apotheosis of the futility of the race He made. The proposition would have been agreed without further words, but that it was desirable that the five millions of inferior listening intellects should understand the decision, and the conclusion from which it came.

The resolution, as first proposed, was adopted with one dissentient, and on the chairman's ruling that this was sufficient to fulfil the condition of unanimity on which the proposition was based, Wyndham understood, from the knowledge of their procedure his brain supplied, that it was an assumption beyond the necessity of words that all must accept the fate for which their own votes had been freely cast. The authority of the assembly would be forthwith used for the prompt and painless end of themselves and their fellow-men. It was that for which they had not the will and sanction alone, but the ample power, and from which only such as he would have further freedom of choice, from the moment the resolution had been proclaimed.

CHAPTER FOUR

When Wyndham Smith, ranking fourth among the intellects of the world by the right of his Colpeck brain, had listened to the monotonous assents of the ninety-six voices that had preceded his own, his eyes had followed the repeated question down the farther side of the table, looking without curiosity at faces he knew before, of men and women whose lives were as empty, their characters as colourless, as was his own in this alien personality that he had so strangely acquired.

It was not likely that he should regard with particularity a girl of no more than twenty-three years at the far end of the table, who was placed as ranking fifty-seventh among this intellectual aristocracy to which she belonged.

Yet his eyes had lingered a moment, his emotion stirred to admiration at a hint of vivacity, a difference of animation which lit the cold, sad beauty of her face, and subtly separated it from the equally regular profiles of other women who sat above or below her. The moment of interest, of admiration—it was no longer than that—was of the ego of Wyndham Smith, and was countered by the protest of the Colpeck brain, which had been taught to view her with a faint disfavour, being the strongest emotion it was accustomed to experience, and which also knew the vague suspicion, and the definite taboo, which divided her from the expected destiny of the women of her generation.

The Colpeck brain, had it concentrated upon her sufficiently, hearing the toneless assent she gave to the verdict of common death might have thought that there were few among the five millions of mankind—to be exact, no more than forty-four others—who would be so certain to cast their votes in the same scale.

For at the time of her birth the settled peace of the world had been stirred and shocked by the discovery of a monstrous crime. A woman who could not have been very far from her fiftieth year, and who had borne in her youth the three children allowed by law, had actually contributed three further children to the nurseries of the race.

It was a monstrosity against which no precautions were taken, since at this period any initiative of criminality had long left the world. It was discovered only by, unlikely accident, shortly after the birth of the third—being, actually, the woman's sixth—child. It stirred the emotions of men at once to horror and fear, as it would have seemed unlikely that they would ever be moved again, like the last ripple of a tide that was settling to eternal quiet. The woman's death was quickly agreed, as a warning, however needless, to other lawless impulses which might linger among mankind.

The deaths of three children were decreed with a more urgent necessity, for ancient wisdom had taught that it is among the later children whom a woman bears that there will be found the firebrands who scorch their kind. Indeed, it was only after the establishment of the custom of limiting children that the world could be observed to approach steadily to the placid harbour in which it was anchored now.

But here a difficulty arose. The fourth and fifth children, having been registered and branded in the usual routine of the common nursery, were identified and eliminated without difficulty. But the mother had unfortunately had some hours of warning before the discovery of her criminality had been finally demonstrated, during which she had contrived to change her just-born child with some other, so that, after the most exhaustive investigation, there had still remained forty-five girl-children of whom it was impossible to say with certainty that any one might not be the sixth offspring of the woman's most lawless blood. Faced with this position, the wisdom of the race, putting passion aside, had preferred the lesser evil, and had offered her pardon if she would identify the issue of her iniquity. But this, with an unrepentant obstinacy, she had declined to do; and when every resort of ingenuity had been exhausted in the endeavour to discover the secret which she concealed (or which, indeed, it is a more probable supposition was no longer hers, owing to the method she had employed for mixing the children), she was reluctantly executed.

After the first sound and natural impulse to destroy the forty-five infants among whom the one unfit for life had been inextricably mingled had been debated, it was weakly resolved, and may be regarded as indicative of the decadence of a failing world, to let them live, under some disabilities of education and other experiences, with the condition that they should not be allowed, on reaching the age of maturity, to contribute to the usual quota of babies, so that the disturbing element might not take evil root in the generation to come.

But, in spite—unless it were because?—of the disabilities they had experienced, when, on the commencement of their twentieth year, they had been intellectually graded by the usual perfect and impartial method, it was found that they were of a most unusual average intelligence, so that though the one already mentioned was actually ranked among the first hundred of the five millions of mankind, the suspicion which this circumstance must have fixed upon her was mitigated by the fact that several others, all of whom could not be of abnormal ancestry, were almost equally eminent.

To the first proposal of universal euthanasia there were few who had responded with a more ready affirmative than had Vinetta (a name which, individual and with no following numerals, proclaimed her, in spite of the recognition of her intellectual status, as outcast among her kind), which is not surprising in consideration of the life of watchful repression which had been hers since, as a child of three, she had overheard the remark of a female keeper: "That's the one, if you ask me; the little misborn girl."

From that hour she had moved and spoken in cautious dread lest some development of character, even some trick of gesture, might betray her, as having been that of the mother whom, with a growing confidence, she believed to have been her own. For who could say that the doom which had been suspended before might not still fall upon her, if her development should appear to supply sufficient evidence of the parent from whom she came? Her own destruction, and the release of her companions from disabilities which were not justly theirs, might have been considered measures of an equal and obvious equity.

So she had moved, watchful, imitative, among the tepid emotions of aimless, emulationless, dreadless surrounding lives, till the hints of her unwary childhood were forgotten or negatived by the restraints and repressions of later years. Saved from sourness or malignity of temper by a nature which would have been buoyant, joyous, adventurous, in more normal circumstances, her thoughts were yet darkened by the bitter knowledge of her mother's murder, and by a mental aloofness, half hatred and half contempt, towards the civilization which she had entered through no legal door.

Of all the millions who were united in passive recognition of the fact that their uncoloured lives had drifted into a calm that was worse than wreck, she may have been the only woman whose heart beat hard at times with a rebellion she dared not show. She assented at once to the Colpeck project, not as thinking it a gesture by which the Creator must take rebuke, but rather as one which He would accept with the same willingness as herself, and with entire approval of the self-judgment by which the human race had saved Him the trouble of staging their appropriate end.

When Wyndham Smith had proposed his second objection to the resolution, her heart had leaped to a sudden hope, which might, in a different environment, have given birth to incautious words. But she was saved from that by the custom which discouraged unpondered speech, and by the repressions of two decades.

The quick hope had died as she had silently recognized the absence of response among those around her, and then—at last had leaped again to the flame of wild audacity of which she saw that she must not give the faintest sign. Inwardly she congratulated herself on the wisdom of her earlier silence, for it was clear that the resolution would only have been accepted in the form in which it was finally passed with the certain confidence that one man alone would elect to live—even if he would do so after considering the solitude which would be before him, with the discomforts which his isolation would inevitably involve.

She did not dare to look up the table to Wyndham Smith, lest their eyes should meet and her glance betray to others the emotions she must not show. She sat passive, with downcast eyes, striving to isolate herself in her own thoughts, and as she reflected thus there came a doubt, and a quietening fear.

Welcome as the proposal had been, gladly as she would have accepted the adventure of living in the old dangerous, doubtful ways, she did not like the direction from which it came. She had a special aversion, not to this Colpeck alone, but to the whole Colpeck clan. It was a Colpeck who had been active in the investigation which had exposed her mother's escapade, and another Colpeck who had proposed the verdict by which she died. It was peculiarly the Colpeck policies, the Colpeck attitude, which had brought her race to this point from which it sought escape by the road of death. Passion towards an individual, either of hate or love, she had been taught to regard as a vulgar criminality such as had long ceased to degrade her kind. But she knew herself to have many criminal impulses which she dared not show. Her existence was an impropriety in itself. She had the lawless mind, the unnatural emotions of a sixth child: she had the blood of one who had played the outlaw among her kind.

Now she thought to make secret approach to the one man who refused the wisdom of all his race, and, in doing this, to flout their will, even as her mother had done before, and as he had no purpose to do. What he did— whether he should stand out, or cease to oppose that which he could not stay—would be done with the permission of all. What she would propose to him would be to make derision of the gesture of refusal which they had planned to make in the face of God, so that it might rouse no more than derisive laughter in the Heaven which they defied.

Like her mother, she would declare lonely war upon the will and wisdom of all her kind, but now in a larger way, by which she might defeat the settled purpose of all. Was it to this great end that she was born, and that her mother had sinned? But—what would a Colpeck say? Might he not decline the offer with horror or contempt? She felt that this was what the Colpeck who was fourth in the intellectual order—the Colpeck of yesterday—would be likely to do. He was not one to condone anything of a lawless kind. And she felt that he disliked and distrusted in his tepid way, as she disliked him with the pulse of a freer blood. She wished it had been almost any but he. But—the Colpeck of yesterday? He had seemed somewhat different in the last hour. And then she remembered—and it was then that she was aware of a sharp fear—where the difference lay, she knew that the hours of sleep of the coming night were to see the reversal of the operation of the night before. The ego of the primitive man which now ruled over the Colpeck brain would be restored to the savage from whom it came, and he would be returned to his own time, with no more than the vexation of a dream that he could not clearly recall. The restored Colpeck ego would be able to review the memory of what he had thought and said today, but would he approve and adopt? It was doubtful—or it might be said that it was less likely than that. It was an improbable thing. Vinetta went to her own room with sombre and thoughtful eyes.

CHAPTER FIVE

Wyndham Smith—or let us say the body that had been his when he walked in another world—paced with a restless impotence the limits of that confining room, which it seemed that those who would visit him could enter or leave at will, but which met him at every point with smooth, impenetrable walls, through which he could find no breach.

He knew—for he had been told, and he half believed—that he was no more than the one-day occupant of a body that was not his; that this strange-seeming environment was his familiar home; and the memories, that seemed so natural and so near, were no more than those of an alien ego, which himself had never experienced, and which tomorrow would be outside his knowledge or recollection, when he should have resumed control of his native body and brain.

He half believed—indeed, more than half—for his memory revealed that which had been spoken in this same room on the previous night, when it had been Wyndham Smith himself who had listened and made response. And, beyond that, he was conscious of some discords of feeling and judgment, some reluctances of his own ego to accept the explosive standards of life and conduct which were approved by the brain which he now controlled. Without knowledge or memory of the life of the world which was round him now, he felt, though he was debarred from its actual contact or sight, that he would control the body of Wyndham Smith to somewhat different purposes than those which had produced the accumulated experiences of which he was conscious now. He was roused from these thoughts by a woman's voice.

"I suppose," it said, "you do not know who I am?"

He turned to see a girl's form, with a face the beauty of which was saddened by a shadow of self-restraint, even of self-repression, but was yet serene, as being assured of its own efficiency to meet the challenge of life in whatever form. The shadow was not one that would have been seen except by one who looked with the eyes of another world. "No," he said, with a slow deliberation, "I do not know you at all."

"So," she said, speaking as slowly as he had done, though from a different cause, for she was using language which was strange to her, and she saw that the error of but one word might be fatal to all she hoped—"so I supposed it would be. Yet you know enough to guess that you may have seen me with other eyes."

"Yes, I can guess that."

"Yet" she went on, "it is as strangers that we must meet now. Do you think me one who would be likely to lie?"

He weighed the slow gravity of her speech with such wits as he had, and in the light of the experiences of Wyndham Smith in another world. He looked into eyes of a very clear grey, under darker brows, which it would be easier to love than to disbelieve.

"No," he said, "I do not think you would lie."

"Then I can say that which would give life to me, and, it may be, also to you. Do you wish to die, either in your own body, or in that which you now wear?"

"No," he said, "I would rather live." In the body of Wyndham Smith there could be no doubt about that.

"Then if you will listen to me, you may both live, as may I. I should warn you first that you must not mention that I have been here, from whatever cause. It would be fatal to me, and to that body to which you may return at your next sleep, nor could I say what result it would have to that in which you are now. But I tell you that which must be known by the brain which you now rule, for its use at a later time."

She went on in clear, careful, unemotional words, and with an economical brevity of explanation that allowed no obtrusive detail to obscure the outline of that which she had to say. She told of the conditions of life in her own world, and the despair which had risen at last into a common resolve to end the appalling quiet of its stormless seas. She told of how the ego which had belonged to the body of Wyndham Smith had inspired that into which it had been transferred to a rejection of what would else have been no less than the universal will. She told of other things which it is needless to detail here.

She said at last, "What I must ask you is this, and you must know that the choice is yours, for I will have nothing done by a trick, or against your will. Would you retain the body you now have, or resume that which was yours till the last hour, of which I have told you all that I can in a little space? And before you answer that, I would show you my own fear that if you should return to the brain and body you had before, you may lack the resolution to take the hard path of continuing life, which it is my purpose to share."

"I do not think you need fear that."

"Yet I do; and, if you feel that you love life, you may fear it for yourself. For you must consider that you had no will to make stand against the common resolve, when you had that body before."

The Colpeck ego that was in the body of Wyndham Smith considered this. He could not think that he would embrace death in a needless way; yet the argument had a force that he could not deny, and he would be fool indeed if he should ask his return to a body that lacked courage to guard the existence he valued now. And he thought that, whether this were a real danger or not, it was a transfer of very doubtful advantage to him. Now that he had the knowledge and memories that were Wyndham Smith's, he knew that he had a good life, and one to be guarded with care, even though it might have its pains, its perils, its frustrations and toils. The alternative of a time which had become so barren of pain and grief that men had come to an end of joy would have had little allure, even without the further knowledge that this life was, at the best, to be cast aside for an experimental solitary reversion to more primitive things.

"I am content," he said, "to be where I am, and to go thus to the backward days, if you can bring it to that."

Vinetta was glad to hear him say that, for it took her forward a short way on her chosen road, but she was not greatly surprised, and she knew that the part that was still ahead was of a more dangerous kind, and might be far harder to win.

"I can promise nothing," she said; "for it must be arranged, if at all, so that he will also agree, to whom I must go now. I must talk to him in a straight way, as I have done here, and what I offer he may refuse and perhaps denounce. But I shall not be easy to thwart, for I try for a stake which is great to me, being a better life than I thought ever to have, besides that it will bring that which my mother did to a great end, such as she would have been glad to foresee.

"As for you, if I fail, you will know well enough, when those who have charge will come to put you to sleep as they did before; but if I succeed, I suppose that you may go to sleep when you next will; and, beyond that, you will know nothing at all."

Having said that, she went, with no further words or regard for him whom she left behind, with whom she had no concern, whether for evil or good. Except that she had a bitter thought: "He is Colpeck still, in whatever body he be, it is all one; and he had no liking for me, for the dream that we two might have been as one in a world alone, though it stirred (in a faint way) the body which another ego had ruled, left him cold of soul, as he ever was.

"Am I the only one of my race who has living blood? And will the new ego that is in the Colpeck body today be of strength to rouse it to better ends, or will its own cowardice prevail, when he considers what may be the toils of a lonely life? Will he be glad of the offer I make, as giving comradeship, and a further hope than could be his, if they should leave him alone? Or will his brain still work in the Colpeck way, so that he will see outrage in the lawless course by which I think to mock the will of the race, and make Heaven's jest of that which they seek to do?

"Well, it will be soon known, and if I fail, we must all go to the common doom; for there has been enough of the life we live. They are right in that, having weighed themselves, as I think, in a true scale."

With these thoughts she went. As for Wyndham Smith, he waked in his bed, being aware that he had slept too long, for broad daylight was in the room.

"I have had," he said, "a most silly dream."

And, if, after that day, he was somewhat different from what he had been before, and ordered his life to more futile ends, it was no more than may often be seen, that men will change as the years go by; and there may be many reasons for that, and among them one that we do not guess.

CHAPTER SIX

Vinetta knew that what she did next must be at some risk to herself, but it was the path to the sole hope that she had. Nor may the risk at this stage have been very great. She had the advantage of being under no suspicion at all. Her lawless birth (which was no more than a doubt against which the odds were forty-four to one) had long ceased to be questioned, in view of the discretions of recent years.

And her own vote had been given in the popular, expected direction. Nor did suspicion readily stir among those who, however intellectually eminent they might be in comparison with their contemporaries, had long ceased to be alert to the possibilities of rebellion in a world where lawless impulses had become as rare as noxious weeds in their glasshouses of husbandry.

Her dread was less that she might be observed to seek conference with Colpeck-4XP than that she might fail to persuade him to what she would.

She knew that the operation which would restore the twentieth-century ego to its barbarous body would be timed for eight A.M., and would involve preparations by which its subjects would be isolated for a previous hour. It was shortly after nine when she returned to her own apartment, after visiting the body of Wyndham Smith. She had chosen a time at which she had known that the routines of her own companions, which were of an absolute regularity, would secure her from observation.

Now she would wait until ten, at which hour the ninety-nine other members of her hundred (and therefore the co-occupants of a single residence) would be engaged at their solitary meals. She was of a disposition to outrage convention, and test the quality of this alien ego, by visiting Colpeck-4XP at a time which would certainly be unobserved, but which would be considered fundamentally indecent by any human being now living, except perhaps herself—she was less than sure of that—and, even more doubtfully, him.

But she would try. And if he should refuse to talk under such conditions, or to be observed during the taking of food, he might, at least, understand that there must be urgent cause for such an intrusion and consent to meet her at a later hour, for which there would still be time. And that decision gave her a clear period of leisure in which to arrange her own thoughts; to face boldly her lawless desires, and the criminalities by which she contemplated their re-alization; and to order the arguments by which she must endeavour to win this alluringly barbarous stranger who had come into possession of Colpeck body and Colpeck brain to co-operate with her.

And as she thought during the next hour, her mind busy with many arguments and doubts, many speculations and fears, she would have said that she was oppressed by the greatest trouble her life had known, which would be hard to deny, she being faced by the twilight of all her race, and with no more than precarious hope of avoiding the common death. Yet the fact was that she had been waked to a more vivid mood than she had known in the years behind. Life roused itself at the nearness of death, as, in those who deserve its boon, it will ever do. If she had more fear than her life had known till that hour, she had also more active hope. Fear and hope fed from the same dish, on which they equally thrived. She had more fear than when she had voted for her own end, for resignation was gone.

There came a time when her evening meal slid on to the table, as it would ever do at the same hour, by which she knew that the time for which she waited had come.

She must not stay to eat, though the routines of life had become so absolute that she had a puzzled wonder as to what the consequences of such abstention might prove to be. She rose at once from the pneumatic couch on which she had reclined in the relaxation of thought, and made a way to the apartment of Colpeck-4XP which no bolts obstructed, and which was independent of opening doors.

The solidity of matter, which had been an accepted faith of the nineteenth century, had become, in the twentieth, more or less theoretically denied or experimentally refuted, without being recognized for the utter delusion which it was subsequently demonstrated to be.

It was recognized as a mathematical possibility that, as an atom consists of molecules as far apart from one another, and relatively as small, as the planets of the solar system, if each of these molecules should be themselves of no greater density, nor composed of more solid particles, then, if the universe were compressed to an absolute solidity, it might—even on the assumption that the material has objective reality—be compressed into less space than is now occupied by a pin's head: but this knowledge was incomplete and unapplied.

Vinetta (avoiding the sliding rails by which the food-machines and other services did their silent, punctual work) walked through walls that were opaque to sight, and contained sound, but were no hindrance to her, or to the purple garment she wore. The privacies of the world which Vinetta knew were not secured by bolt or lock, but by an iron rule of routine, which had become stronger than any law.

Now she made a circuitous way through rooms which would be vacant at such an hour, and walked at last, with a quiet face, but a fast-beating heart, into the one she sought.

"Do you mind," she asked, "if I talk to you now? It is important—to me," Colpeck-4XP had been sucking mixed fruit-juices through a tube, in small quantities, at the regulation intervals. A plate of some pink substance which, apart from its colour, had the appearance of grated cheese, stood before him to be eaten later. He looked up astonished, perhaps repelled, by this invasion, unprecedented not merely in his individual experiences but in the records of eccentricity or crime during several previous centuries.

"I shouldn't have come without cause," she said uncertainly, controlling with difficulty the desire to withdraw from the sight of another human being absorbing drink.

"No," he agreed dubiously. "I suppose not." He had ceased to drink. He laid down the glass tubes. Her sense of having outraged both his modesty and her own diminished somewhat with this cessation, though, as his eyes met hers, she could not control a blush such as may not have been observed for three hundred years on a woman's face.

"I haven't come to Colpeck-4XP," she went on, bravely ignoring her burning cheeks, "but to Wyndham Smith."

That was what she had resolved to and it seemed to have some effect.

"Yes," he said, though still in that dubious puzzled voice. "There is that. But why have you come?"

"I went to see Colpeck-4XP," she answered, "an hour ago."

"You—yes, I see. But why?"

"He will be willing to remain in his present body, if you concur."

The information was of a nature to cause Wyndham Smith, now that the first shock of traditional unseemliness was over, to forget the circumstances in which they met.

He had been thinking rather sombrely, during the last hour, of the alternatives that lay before him—either to return to a barbarous, bloody world of which he had no recollection now, and of which he could only form a vaguely terrible picture, or to face the utter loneliness of a deserted earth, with no better prospect than solitary death at last, which would end his species with himself—one of these—or else to join the general euthanasia which was the deliberately selected doom of his fellow men.

But the actual choice he had supposed to be even less than that. The accepted rule was that a transferred identity must be adjusted within two days unless *both* the egos concerned should prefer to continue in their exchanged tenements, and such an occurrence had never been. Was it likely *now*?

The information she brought gave him a choice which he might not have had, and which might not be easy to make. It was welcome news. But it explained nothing. Before he discussed, he must understand. "Why," he asked, "did you get him to tell you that?"

"Because it was essential for me to know whether, if I should agree on something with you tonight, I should have to deal with someone else tomorrow."

Yes. He saw that. That was sense. But what bargain could she wish to make? "To what," he asked, "do you want me to agree?"

"Before I say that, will you tell me whether you mean to go back to the other life?"

"It sounds the most natural thing to do."

"History tells us that it was very horrible. Pain. Heat. Cold. Quarrels. Bad food. Diseases. All sorts of muddle and dirt. Even insects under your clothes."

"We haven't decided that this life is any good."

"But that must have been worse in ever so many ways."

"And yet people wished to live."

"But you are going to live. You've arranged that."

"Not in a very attractive manner."

"Then it is just to oblige Colpeck-4XP to come back to that, if he thinks even the twentieth century wouldn't be so bad? It's you who've done that for him, and then you won't face it yourself."

"That's foolish. He can end his life here, if he will. He'll be no worse off than he was before. In fact, better. I've given him a chance that he wouldn't have had the initiative to get for himself."

This was a disconcerting reply. She had hoped something from this argument of justice, knowing that the brain which Wyndham Smith now controlled was of a particular scrupulosity on points for honour. But his reply was difficult to rebut. She had a better hope when he added, "But I haven't said yet that I won't let him have his way."

She said, "There won't be much pleasure in being the only creature alive, even though the machines go on working, as I suppose they will, more or less"

"I doubt that. No. I don't see that there will."

Their eyes met. Prompted by the insurgent ego of twentieth-century barbarism which now controlled it, the brain of Colpeck-4XP became alive to the implication of this amazing interview.

"Suppose," she said, refusing to withdraw the gaze which he met so disconcertingly, "that you were not quite alone?"

He did not affect to misunderstand. He answered directly, "You could not do that, even if I would agree—if you would dare. You have voted for your own death."

"But I was the rebel child."

It was an audacious assertion, even though it might be a true guess. Yet what penalty could it now bear, even though it were believed, even though it should be broadcast to the 4,999,998, who would be shocked by its shameless boast? There can be little for fear or hope, for resentment or retribution, among those who have united to end their race.

After this, there were some minutes of silence. The ego of Wyndham Smith warred with the brain, the acquired character, the traditions of Colpeck-4XP, and the conflict was confused beyond speedy determination or assurance of victory for either side.

Vinetta understood something of this. She judged correctly that to ask too much at this moment might be to get nothing at all, which she must not risk.

But these new sharp emotions of hope and doubt had a fighting quality which would not be still. She asked, "You will not go back?"

He considered this. "No," he said, with deliberation. "I will stay here. I will see it out. That is, if he agrees."

"He will agree," she said confidently. Her voice had a note of victory, of exaltation, such as had not been heard for centuries from a human throat.

With cautious boldness, she pushed forward her lines of attack, asking more, though much less than all. "You will not expose me that I have come here?"

No," he answered, with the same reluctant-seeming deliberation as before, as though being forced along a path that he feared to tread, "I will not do that."

"I wish," she said, "you would eat. Why should you stay for me? It is I, not you, who transgress. The time is short now. You will miss your meal."

"So," he answered, "will you." He added, "I cannot eat while you are here. It is not done."

She saw, as he said this, that he waged a fight which she must help him to win. She must not forget that he was handicapped with a Colpeck brain, or rather with one that had been trained to value the Colpeck traditions, cautions, and inhibitions.

She said, "There was a time when men ate in each other's presence."

"There was a time," he replied, "as you have reminded me, when insects might crawl upon human flesh." His hand made a spasmodic shrinking movement as he said this. It was a vile thought for one before whose birth most insects had left the world.

"There was a later time when it became a marriage custom to eat together, though all other men, except young children, would feed apart."

"But," he replied, "that custom is long since dead in more decent times. It is left behind."

She asked, "Where will our customs be in a week's time? We do well to boast! But there will be one custom that is ended now."

She reached over. She took his spoon. She ate a mouthful of food. After that, she went with averted eyes.

Neither did he look at her. They were both ashamed at what she had done. But she had raised a chaos within his heart that he could not still.

CHAPTER SEVEN

"I am not Colpeck-4XP. I am Wyndham Smith." So he told himself a score of times as he paced his room during the night, sometimes in explanation, sometimes in self-excuse, sometimes in the endeavour to mould desire to the point of settled resolve.

Yet it was hard to realise, if not to believe. Its truth was evident in the fact alone that he was awake and disturbed with conflicting thoughts. Every memory, every tradition of conduct, every argument with which his mind was stored was on the side of the race to which he was otherwise so remote, yet which, by one irrevocable word, had become his in its hour of death.

He saw that he had three questions to vex his mind, of which he must dispose in an orderly rotation:

(1) Did he really intend to survive the general race-suicide which he had been solitary to oppose?

(2) If so, did he wish Vinetta to be his wife in the future days?

(3) If he did, was there any possible method by which she could escape the common fate, after she had consented thereto?

He saw that, if he should answer the first question in the negative, the other two did not arise, and that it should therefore have prior consideration. Similarly, if the second should be negatived, the third need not be asked, and that was further evidence that he had numbered them rightly.

Yet their precedence was less simple than that, for, had the first stood alone, he would have had a week for its leisured consideration, whereas an affirmative answer to the second might entail prompt action in various ways, so that, for its sake, the prior question must be promptly resolved.

Again, the reply to the second might be influenced by those which could be given to the other two, so that, at the last, he saw that he must reverse their order. As he debated these questions, he saw, more clearly than he had done before, the fundamental upheaval of all the habits and experiences of life, as he had hitherto lived it, which a lonely survival would mean; which, in most ways, would be little different if the survivors were two.

Vaguely, he saw that the machines must go—that fertility must be released, to recapture an earth from which it had been driven as an insanitary, obscene, insubordinate force, too barbarous for modern man to endure. The results of such changes must be beyond the forecasting of human wit. A new balance of nature must be established. It might not occur without much wastage, amidst which his own life, or that of his children, might be overwhelmed. He had thought that, whether there should be one or two that survived, there would be no more than minor resulting differences. And so, in many ways, it must be.

But with the thought of children, he observed one enormous variation. If he were to survive alone, it could but defer for a few more years the final passing of the race of men from the earth which they had lacked wisdom to make a tolerable home. But if there were two—that would be, indeed, to mock the whole purpose of this gesture by which man was to reject the gift of life, casting it back with contempt at the feet of God. Suppose the two who lived should found, to better purpose, a better race? Those who died might be judging themselves rather than their Creator, and their verdict might not be wrong.

As he thought this, the brain of Colpeck-4XP, driven by the ego of Wyndham Smith, stirred itself to a passionate hope, to hard resolve. It roused itself to a great game, which must be played for the greatest stake that a man could have. And the mere thought of taking on such conflict against fate, and against his kind, brought a sense of bewildering freedom, of escape from the smooth, soft, eventless servitude which had gained no more than the absence of all the adverse impacts which had pained or thwarted those heroic ancestors who had endured under different skies. He saw that, in a blind folly, man had sought to change the nature and purpose of human life, saying that it was evil only of which they would make an end, and, arm-in-arm, good and evil together had left the world.

From many conflicting thoughts he was aware of one resolution finally formed. He would live, if he could—with her.

Would he live alone? He was less sure. He was less inclined to that than before. After this new dream, it had a barren, abortive aspect which he would be tardy to choose.

Could he contrive that not only his life, but hers should endure? It was hard to see how that could be done. Yet a way there must surely be. But first he would communicate with him who now had the body of Wyndham Smith—which it was not easy to think that any would wish to hold—and agree that they should continue as they now were.

From the high dream he had had, he came to a sharp fear that this agreement would not be made; but he found that Vinetta had been right about that, for the ego of Colpeck-4XP was content to flee from a dying world to one which was more familiar to the brain that now served its will.

CHAPTER EIGHT

Wyndham Smith—as it may be preferable to call him, if it be allowed that the ego is more than the body in which it dwells—did not sleep till late, and waked some minutes after the universal hour. It was a fault of routine which it would have been his normal duty to report to the physician of his hundred, who would have examined him, and either rebuked whatever deviation of conduct might have caused this eccentricity, or recommended either an immediate operation, or an early visit to the nearest euthanasia furnace if he had observed any indication of failing health; for it had long been an axiom of worldly wisdom that, however absolute the control of pain might have become, the beginning of a disease is the better end of it at which to die.

But even the most docile member of the community might have felt it needless to take such precaution when it was understood that the thousand of such refuges which the world contained were to be visited by the whole of its inhabitants in a week's time. To Wyndham Smith it came as no more than a moment's recollection of the precepts that childhood learned, to be rejected in the instant that followed. The illegality which he had in mind was more serious in itself, and less to be condoned by the resolution that the last night's council had taken. He waited until the hour of the morning meal arrived, drank and ate with a brevity which would leave him a clear forty minutes free from fear of interruption in what he did, and went to Vinetta's room.

Having reached it, he knew that he had come to a place where no one would intrude unasked, if the present order should continue for many years; nor could those who were within be seen or overheard. These personal rooms, with their opaque though penetrable walls, were the only real privacies that the earth contained at a time when any sound, near or far, excepting themselves, could be picked up by a million receivers, if they should chance to be directed upon the area from which it came.

His caution must be that he should not exceed his time, and that Vinetta should neither be observed to be in consultation with him, nor to neglect the normal occupations that passed the tedium of her waking hours.

She looked up as he entered with sudden joy, her eyes shone with something of the buoyant courage of youth, meeting in his own an excitement, if not an elation, that equalled hers, for she guessed at once what his coming meant, and that the first battle was almost won.

She said, "I was sure you would. I have not let myself doubt. Not even when I was most afraid in the night."

He answered gravely, but with the same buoyancy in his voice and the thought he spoke, "Yesterday it was five millions to one. We have halved it now! But we must not think that it will be easy to do."

Her bowl of food was half-emptied. She pushed it towards him with its single spoon. She said, "You must eat with me. You reckon well. But you must not call us two. We are one from now."

He took up the spoon, but not as readily as she would have liked, so that she added, "It is no more than your custom was."

"Yes," he agreed, with a puzzled look, as of one who strives to recall a forgotten dream, "I suppose it was." He put the spoon to his mouth. But having taken this in a ritual way, he pushed the bowl back. "I had some," he said, "before I came here. I need not rob you of food. I have come to talk."

"So we must," she agreed. "And they will not guess. It would be useless to propose that they leave me alive. They would never consent to that."

"No. They would destroy you at once, if they had the least suspicion of what we plan. They would tell the machines. After the vote you gave, they would have all men's support."

She knew that to be true. The order of the First Hundred would be obeyed by those who attended on the machines, and the automata had a terrible power. It would be useless to evade or resist. They both knew that; too surely for the wasting of words.

She asked, thinking of the machines, "Will they order them to destroy themselves, or will they let them go on?"

"I have wondered that. But we shall hear. As I am to remain alive, they may be willing to consult my preference in what they do."

"I suppose that, as orders are issued by our Hundred alone, they may decide that we who belong thereto shall be the last to remain alive."

"So we must hope that they will. But I cannot urge it. It is not my concern. And it might be unwise that it should be proposed by you."

"We must hope that its wisdom will be seen by others."

"But even so—"

"Yes. They are sure to require the whole of us to enter together. But we have time to devise a plan."

"So we must. It was a foolish thing that I proposed— that sterilizing of the sea. I did not foresee that the discussion would develop the way it did."

"Yes. But there is one thing sure. It cannot be done in a week. I wonder how Pilwin-C6P will get over that?"

"He may propose that the machines be so directed that they will continue whatever he may require them to do. There would be no difficulty there."

She looked at him with startled eyes, guessing his thought. "And you might stop them when all but ourselves were dead? *You would interfere with the machines?*"

Her voice shook now with a fear with which she had been hypnotized from her childhood's days. It was such as the twentieth century could only partially understand. A child who attempted to embrace a dynamo's armature would certainly have been pulled away: it would not have been encouraged to put its head under a steam-hammer, or to fondle a chaff-cutter, and there were some factory laws

for the fencing off of machines of particularly bad reputa-
tion, as savage animals at a zoo might be barred from the
public reach. But the machines of that day were primitive
in character, most of them capable of nothing more than
one operation monotonously repeated, and generally even
that would require the constant watchfulness of a human
colleague. They were unable to feed each other. Some of
them were even unable to oil themselves.

Naturally with the passing centuries, changes came.
The machines of this day had become automatic, large and
small, capable of many complicated operations, and
though without any originating intelligence, yet able to act
upon intelligent directions in sustained, discriminating
ways.

It was nearly seven hundred years since the genius of
the Japanese designer, Hirato, had utilized the sense of
smell for the extermination of the Asian tiger. He devised
small, crawling, automatic machines with strong steel-
toothed jaws, which would follow any strong scent to
which they were introduced, and let them loose on the tiger's tracks. A second machine, set on the same track as
the first, with an hour's interval, might lead a long way or
short, but would be likely to come at last to a place where
a tiger had struck impotently at a cold, hard, crawling
beast that nuzzled maddeningly into his side, and the re-
lentless jaws, roused by the blows, had snapped back with
a grip they would not loose until that into which they bit
had left them quiet for a long hour, which no living, tor-
tured tiger could be expected to do.

That had been a novelty then. There was even an old
painting extant which showed the last tigers collected on a
little tableland to which the machines could not climb, and
about forty of these implacable, single-purposed automata
ringing them round, and waiting with unrelenting patience
to resume their tireless, sleepless pursuit, when despera-

tion or the pangs of thirst should madden the beasts to bound over them and continue their futile flights.

It was by means of many variations and extensions of this idea, aided by the use of disease viruses of many kinds, that sentient life had been almost completely destroyed upon the land-surfaces of the earth, even where they had not been sterilized by wide-spreading layers of concrete which had been poured, like molten lava from huge mountain-side cauldrons set up in Rocky Mountains, Andes, Himalayas, and Alps, and forming, as they solidified, hard crusts in which no life could root, and through which none could pierce upward to find the sun.

The machines of this day were, or had been in past centuries, initiated by human thought. They carried out the orders the First Hundred, as they were interpreted to them by lesser men. But they did this with little present interference. They designed and constructed each other. They prepared and supplied themselves with the fuel which they required. Their operations were so extensive, so interdependent, so fundamental, that any ill-formed or unauthorized interference might have incalculable and disastrous results. It was one of the first nursery lessons that nothing could excuse tampering with a machine, or obstruction of its operations. To forget this was the one unpardonable delinquency for which the punishment would be instant death.

So it had been understood. It was a law which had taken no toll of the present generation of human lives, for it had been universally obeyed. The inhibition had become too strong to be broken at any likely occasion. When Vinetta exclaimed, in a troubled half-incredulous wonder of realization, *"You would interfere with those machines?"* Wyndham understood very well the instinctive terror that shook her mind. But he was already resisting the impulses of his new brain more instantly, more successfully, than he had at first been able to do. The knowledge that he had only just come into control of that which another had assembled and moulded was sufficient to encourage him to question its precepts, unless they were suggested to him with clear reason in their support.

He answered, "I should be cautious in what I did. But one thing is sure. They will be confused, sooner or later, when men are dead. They will end themselves. We should expect that. We should not propose to continue them, which would require knowledge I have not got, and might, in any event, be beyond our power, being no more than two.

"We shall not have the same dread that men have had in the past days lest confusion arise among them, but we must beware that they do us no harm, in a blind way, when they are destroying themselves."

"What a world it will be," she said, "when they have done that! These walls! There will be no houses at all. There will be cold when they have gone! There will be parts of the world, if not all, where we could not live without making heat. We must find how this part would be. Perhaps, if we were near a volcano— They must leave the cars, so that we shall not be kept in one place."

"Yes," he agreed. "We have much to think of. But you must not show that it is of moment to you."

She had, in fact, echoed one of his own thoughts, which had gone farther. They might ask him to choose, before they would become busy to make an end, in what part of the earth he would wish to be. It might be wise—he had some reason to think it would—to choose a spot many thousands of miles away. But to make such a journey, leaving Vinetta behind, would be to make it improbable that they would meet again, even though she should find means to preserve her life when her companions died

Facilities of transport were not numerous in these days. The aeroplane as a means of human transit had been obsolete for three hundred years. What use was there in rising, at foolish peril, into the skies, when you could do nothing at last but come back to earth at the same or another place? It was futility *in excelsis*, and therefore to be rejected even by the most futile age that the earth had seen. For all places of descent had become alike. In a world in which all differences of season or climates had been adjusted, all physical discomforts expelled, and on which vegetation had been largely suppressed, there was little disposition to move about. Oral communication had become absolute over the whole earth. Competition had been eliminated. Occupation had almost entirely ceased. The five thousand communities, each grouped round its central euthanasia furnace, and each housed in ten separate tenements, existed, but did not live.

In contrast to the desire for continual motion which had been the tragic folly of the twentieth century—a period which had honestly and simply believed that the "progress" of humanity would be demonstrated in future years by the ever-increasing speed at which it would whirl about, and which had pledged the sincerity of this curious faith in the blood of a million dead—the final generation of men required a compelling reason for motion rather than for remaining still.

It possessed road-tracks, and a kind of automatic car in which men or goods could be conveyed from one place to another, but these were extensively employed, and most often were clocked out to their destinations without bearing a human occupant.

Wyndham rose. He said, "I must go now. We have seven days. We need do nothing before tonight, when we shall learn more of what the programme will be. After that, I will come again."

"No," she said. "I will come to you."

They parted without meeting of hands or lips, but, with a moment's hesitation, a feeling of awkwardness, of shyness, very strange to themselves, and which was the measure of the novel intimacy which they had established in an age which had become complacent in the belief that it had outmoded love.

CHAPTER NINE

It might have been expected, with some reason in its support, that those who had resolved upon such an act as would destroy not only themselves but the race to which they belonged would have shown symptoms, in the brief interval which remained, of depression, if not despair.

But Wyndham Smith, moving among those who had been the lifelong acquaintances—"friends" would be too warm a word for that tepid relationship—of the body and memories he now possessed, observed an opposite issue. There was slight but definite increase of animation among them, as though, having resolved to die, by the resolution, however faintly, they had come to life—to such life, at least, as they were ever destined to have.

He was conscious also of a lack of the usual cordiality—repulsion would be too strong a word—in their attitude towards himself, which he was at first disposed to attribute to their knowledge that, though he moved with the form and spoke with the memories of Colpeck-4XP, he was actually the strange ego of a distant and most barbarous time. But further reflections and observations showed him that it had a different and deeper cause. It was his decision to live, even in the solitude of an abandoned world, which divided them from him. He experienced something of the loneliness of one who rejects the religion his kindred own.

He would have been more conscious of, perhaps more depressed by, this attitude, had not his mind been sustained by the thought of Vinetta's loyalty, and occupied by vague plans to preserve her life, and equally vague speculations as to what their common future would be likely to be.

So far as he could anticipate the course of events, the coming week would see no change in the eventless routines of life, except such as might be involved in arranging for the general dissolution, and this would require little beyond preparations of the temples of euthanasia for use on a larger scale than that for which they had been designed. There would also be the question of the machines, which, apart from any request from himself, might be left to work out their own destructions, and that of the sterilization of the oceans, for which his own blundering diplomacy was primarily responsible. He supposed that arrangements would be made for the people of each centre to enter the euthanasia furnaces hundred by hundred, the council doing so at the last, when they had assured themselves that not only had the other nine hundred of their community gone on their unreturning journey, but that an enduring silence had settled upon the five thousand centres of human life.

Among that final hundred Vinetta would be expected to take her orderly place in the procession of death. What possible excuse would be accepted? What effectual resistance could be made? What hope was there that the remaining ninety-eight would proceed to an abortive annihilation which would leave her alive to propagate their species anew, and make mockery of their own intention of mocking God? He thought of many devices, many plans, but, so far, only to put them aside. He knew that he had to foil ninety-eight of the best brains in the world, of which three were better than his. He could but hope a woman's wit was working to better purpose than his could do.

He saw that they must depend entirely upon their own resources, for neither he nor she had any personal influence or authority which they could exercise for their own ultimate benefits, apart from the ruling Hundred to which they belonged. Under the urgency of his lawless twentieth-century will, the brain of Colpeck-4XP devised a most cunning idea by which all he sought might have been gained, by an order which was within his personal authority, and would have done all that the occasion required.

The trouble was that it could not be privately issued. It could not be privy to himself and those of lower grade who would accept it from him. For nothing could be privately done. When the First Hundred deliberated, the whole of the world's inhabitants listened in. In fact, everyone could hear everything. The only privacies were in the feeding and sleeping rooms, and there was no possibility of issuing an order during the hours that they were occupied, for everyone was in the same retirement. It would have no reception at all.

Neither was there hope of escape on the earth's surface for Vinetta and himself, even though they could have found means of sustaining life, while facing the hostility of their fellows: not in its most solitary island, its deepest, remotest cave.

There were no lands which heat or cold, deluge or drought, caused to be avoided by social men. Nowhere that would be secure from the iron-toothed automata which would be set to smell their sleeping-couches, then loosed upon them and tirelessly track them down.

Considering the coldness of his reception among those with whom he took the routine exercises of the day, Wyndham was led to wonder whether this feeling might not augment itself during the week to a more active antipathy, and add further danger to a situation already appearing sufficiently ominous. But reflection enabled him to put this doubt confidently aside.

There was not, he concluded, enough of aggressive spirit among this race, self-defeated and self-doomed in its attempt to dodge the divine law that only by opposition is strength sustained, to raise any dangerous heat of animosity against himself. Not even though it should be increasingly realized, as the days passed, that this man who had elected to remain alive was not, in his essential soul, one of themselves, but an alien from a barbarous time.

And their well-trained subordination to restrictive law, all the negative virtues to which they had been moulded by a social order which had no criminal element, no opposition, no rebel motions of any kind, would be sufficient for their restraint.

Though the impulses of his own alien ego contemplated rebellion, he had coolness of judgment to understand how impossible any lawless or separate action would be to these men and women whose lives of negative security had been repeated for centuries in a monotony broken only, as by a long, slow ripple on a surface of windless sea, by the periodic selecting of mates, the preparation of the public nurseries, and the training of a new generation to accept the calm atmosphere of an existence which bartered pleasure for the absence of pain.

A celestial watcher, observing that, as the centuries passed, each of these periods had been approached with a diminishing alacrity, or even a positive and progressive unwillingness to encounter the adventurous responsibilities which they involved, might have seen the logical, inevitable end.

Wyndham Smith concluded that, so long as his compact with Vinetta should remain secret, there would be nothing for himself to fear from his fellow men. But should that be known, there would be no mercy to hope, no defense useful to urge. They would be destroyed together by the cold justice which would hold her to have been bound by her own vote, and it would be a sentence beyond evasion, and without appeal.

But this secret he might hope that they would not learn. Had it not left the problem of saving her own life unsolved, there would have been no more consolation in that.

In such thoughts the day passed, and the hour of the council meeting returned.

CHAPTER TEN

Wyndham Smith took his familiar place with a sense of frustration, of having made a mistake, which was, in itself, an indication of the changed ego which controlled the processes of the Colpeck brain. At intervals during the day, and with increasing inclination during the last two hours, it had occurred to him that it might be advantageous to have a talk with Pilwin-C6P before the council should meet.

It would have enabled him to ascertain what the proposals for the sterilization of the oceans were, and to consider to what extent it would be to his interest to support or accept them. It would be a natural curiosity for him to feel, a natural enquiry to make; and if it should appear to indicate that he was already shaken in his wild intention of surviving his fellow-men—well, there might be no harm in that!

He might even have been able to influence the event, to come to an understanding with Pilwin-C6P in advance of the meeting, upon a matter which, from opposite angles, was of more interest to themselves than to the general body of the community. But he had remembered that Pilwin-C6P was not particularly friendly to himself. Tepidly, they had disliked each other. This feeling stirred in him now with an increased virility. Hesitating, he had let the time pass.

It was a strange feeling to one who had little previous experience of divided will, disturbing his mind with a profundity difficult for one of our habits of indecision to understand. He took his seat now with consciousness of a mental disturbance which, if he should fail to control it firmly, might cause him to betray his alien ego by some abrupt or unseemly word. He looked round on the familiar faces of those who went placidly on their deathward, self-chosen way, with a sense of separation, of latent hostility, which would increase with each passing hour.

Only the thought of Vinetta was potent to balance and restrain his mind, and she was the one whom he must not see.

The chairman commencing without preamble, as the habit was, said first, "To operate the resolution of yesterday, I have had an instruction prepared for your approval. I believe it to be the general desire that our intention should be fulfilled with the dignity of deliberation, but as speedily as may be consistent therewith. It is evident that our thousands cannot terminate themselves simultaneously in a seemly manner. The congestion of the disintegrators would be too great. But in companies of one hundred each, at intervals of twelve hours, it should be possible without exception, at each of the five thousand centres.

"I propose that the order of the procession shall be left for the free determination of each centre, which will naturally consider our and its own convenience in withholding to the last those who are in any way concerned in control or provision of the essential services.

"I propose that the procession shall begin at six A.M. tomorrow, and that the succeeding hundreds shall gain oblivion at intervals of twelve hours thereafter, so that—as we shall necessarily be the last of our own thousand—our own release must be deferred until five days hence at this hour."

Having said this, the chairman waited for about five minutes, during which no one spoke, and after this interval of assenting silence he put the question to each in turn, and the chorus of "I agree"—"I agree" went down the length of the table and came up on the nearer side, until, arriving at Wyndham Smith, the chairman said, "I suppose that you do not vote?" And he replied, "I do not dissent," as he knew that the rules of procedure for such occasions required him to do.

In fact, the resolution was one to which, had it not been liable to misunderstanding, he would have assented with pleasure. It deferred Vinetta's danger until the last, and that with the satisfaction of thinking that the forces of opposition would be diminished by half a million twice daily, until at last they would be a mere half-million to two! And considering how the half-million would be scattered over the earth's surface, and engaged in simultaneous self-destruction, perhaps ninety-eight to two would be a truer arithmetic. With the odds moving so rapidly in the right direction, Wyndham might be excused a moment of satisfaction, feeling the terms of the resolution to be of great importance than the fact that Vinetta, voting for it, had confirmed her assent.

Having disposed of the main proposition with such pleasant unanimity, the chairman came to the further business arising from the resolutions of the previous day.

"It having been resolved," he said, "that we should precede our own departure by doing whatever the circumstances may allow to abate the vexation of life in inferior forms, and in particular from its further gestation in the vast reservoirs of the oceans, and this being a matter on which our brother Pilwin-C6P is our acknowledged authority, it may be convenient to hear his advice thereon."

It was an invitation which appeared to be expected, and to which Pilwin-C6P was quite ready to respond. With no more pause than the etiquette of the assembly required, he proceeded to make a statement delivered in the usual leisurely manner, but with a faintly oracular tone that stirred Wyndham Smith to a fresh antipathy, which he rebuked in vain as evidence of the inability of his barbarous ego to accept the restraints and standards of a more civilized time. Did he wish to be incapable of strong feelings? Even of strong dislikes? He was not sure that he did! But he must cease to debate himself. He must listen. What was the sententious fool saying now?

"We know that life, at least within its own most limited range, which is no more than a short distance above the earth's surface, and a shorter below, has a most insurgent quality. It exists in almost infinite variety, in almost incredible minuteness, in an incalculable number of individual units. It has a persistence and an adaptability very difficult to restrain or overcome.

"Yet...we have found ways. To an extent we have succeeded. If it were practicable to cover the whole surface of land and sea with a coating of concrete no more than two feet in thickness, it is probable that the problem would have been finally solved. But that is not practicable.

"My ancestor, Pilwin-V2H, thought that it could be accomplished other ways. He had a scheme by which at last the earth would have been divested of life, excepting only ourselves, and any inferior organisms which might be required directly for our own use.

"It would be vain to consider now whether, or how far, he were right or wrong. He would have commenced upon the oceans, and the collective wisdom of his contemporaries decided that it was an experiment too hazardous in its results for them to permit.

"But the record of his proposals—of the methods he would have adopted—remains. And the two main objections, which were raised at the time, no longer apply.

"It was said first that the consequences could not be entirely foreseen or controlled, and that they might prove to be inimical to the health or comfort of mankind when the destruction would have reached an irrevocable point. With that opening objection we are no longer concerned.

"It was also urged that the means available were inadequate to the proposed occasion. That view was adopted by a large majority of the council of that time, and may have been right, though it was one with which Pilwin-V2H, and others who specialized in his department, did not agree. But this, again, can give no guidance to us, for we shall be able to utilize machinery which either did not exist at that time, or was required for human service.

"The wind-controls in the polar regions and the Sahara, together with the Australian, Gobi, and Mississippi temperature plants, could all be diverted to this purpose, and would provide a total of sustained efficiency which even the oceans might not be wide or deep enough to resist successfully."

As he ceased, a strange sound came from the lower end of the table, the sound of fear in a human voice. With less than a seemly interval after C6P had spoken, it asked, "You would not release the winds while we still live?"

"No. It would be absurd to propose that. The machinery would be diverted from its present uses on our last day."

A graver, more self-controlled voice asked, "The machinery would continue to operate for a sufficient time?"

"We can see no reason for doubting that. It might continue even until the exhaustion of its sources of power— that is, the deposits of coal and oil that the earth contains."

"In fact," a young man with Arabian features beneath a high forehead, and with eyes of an indescribable sadness, whose position at the chairman's left indicated that he had the second-best intellect in the world, asked languidly, "You would electrocute life?"

"In the oceans. Yes. I do not say that it would be done quickly. But, in the end, yes."

"Why not on land?"

"That might also be possible."

"And in the air?"

"I am less confident about that. But conditions might be made such that it could not endure."

"It has a sound of futility unless it be wholly done."

"The sterilization of the oceans," the chairman interposed, "is a matter on which we are already agreed. We discuss methods only on which we must, as I think, be guided by the advice we have heard. But if it be possible to extend the operations to land and air, it would be in order to propose that."

"So I would," the Arabic-featured one answered, "if it were advised that it could be done."

"I could not promise that," Pilwin-C6P answered frankly, "unless we, or some of us, should remain alive, under less pleasant conditions than we now have, a sufficient time to direct the operations."

This statement was received with a long silence. Across the Arabian face there passed the faint semblance of a mirthless smile. He shook his head, as though at his own thoughts. It was clear that the price was more than any there was disposed to pay.

Wyndham Smith judged that, though the proposal of their deaths had been first made in the form of a gesture of refusal against the unkindly skies, yet they had been impelled to embrace this extremity much less by desire to affront their Creator than by weariness of their own lives.

Vaguely, it gave him a better hope of the issue of the battle he had to win. It encouraged him with the thought that those around him were not greatly concerned in this question of continuing life, and to remember that, but for his own blundering argument, the proposition might not have been considered at all.

"Before," he said, "this proposal be put to a final vote, may I ask how its operations will affect the possibilities of comfortable life on the earth during the coming years on which point you will agree that I have an interest that you do not share?

The question did not meet with an immediate reply, which indeed, by the ordinary procedure, he did not expect; but he felt that it was received, if not with any reaction sufficiently strong to be called hostility, yet with an indifference, an aloofness, which might come to the same result.

"You will observe," the chairman said temperately, breaking the lengthened pause, "that it is by your own desire that you will remain, and if you prefer a course which is contrary to that which will be taken by all your kind, it may not be their first concern to make it easy for you. Yet"—turning to Pilwin-C6P—"it is a question that should, as I see it, be answered plainly."

Pilwin-C6P did not object to do this, but his voice, as he replied, had a faint tone of contempt, as that of one who turns his mind to a small thing. "The earth, as I suppose, will not have much comfort when we are gone. We could not change that, if we would. But it is large for one man. And his lonely life cannot be a matter of much beyond a few weeks—or a few years, if you will. Why should he not go, while he can, to one of the islands in the tropic seas?

"No man has stepped on them perhaps for some hundreds of years, but they will be there still. Their climate will be such that a man's life may endure even though we remove the controls of heat and wind that we now have. And even what we do to the seas will be slow to reach or affect them."

Wyndham Smith listened to this, and thought that he had heard nothing deserving thanks. The idea that he might find a tolerable refuge on one of those remote, abandoned islands had already occurred to his own mind. But, if he should agree to take such a journey, what possibility was there that Vinetta would escape singly and join him there?

Or did he desire that, for their own temporary convenience, they should locate themselves in some solitary place from which they or their descendants would have little hope of reaching a wider world? And an island set in the sea from which life in the coming weeks, or years, was to be electrocuted away, with results incalculable, but certain to be adverse, if not fatal to that island life? There would be no more fish. The fish-eating sea-birds, if any such still lived in those lonely seas, would die. Where would death end?

From wandering into such details his mind was recalled by the fact that another spoke. It was Avanah-F3B, whom he had reason to like. A man seated almost opposite him, of grave placidity, with thoughtful, introspective eyes. His place indicated that he was almost the lowest intellectually, among the First Hundred, but, actually, where there were five million to be graded, there was not much difference in that. He was the chief official historian, his knowledge of the world's past being very great.

He said gently, "If our brother have the great courage to remain alive for a time when he will be the last of his kind, might he not take such control of the machines as the occasion require, so that they may all do that which we aim to reach?"

It was a second suggestion that Wyndham Smith had no pleasure in hearing; but he recognized fairly that it was both reasonable in itself, and likely to arise in the mind of one who regarded the course of human existence as a panoramic whole to which an orderly finish was now being put. His mind, trained in the historical sense, must look with the same curiosity forward as back.

But what should he say in reply? Whatever he might have randomly urged on the previous day, he had no desire for the policy of sterilization to succeed—certainly no wish to assist it. And he was, by his personal predilection, as well as by his acquired proclivities, of a scrupulous honour, which would object, even at this emergency, to pledge itself to that which it would not do.

The chairman was acute enough to perceive the hesitation which delayed his reply, and gave it a natural interpretation. "It may be," he said, "that Colpeck-4XP is not finally resolved that he will live a solitary life when all his kind will have left the earth. If that be so, it becomes a pledge that he could not give."

Wyndham Smith saw that he must speak. Certainly it was a pledge that he would not give. Was it one that, apart from the doubt which had been suggested, he could directly refuse? How would such a refusal be received? But was there really a doubt? Suppose that Vinetta should falter, after further consideration of the hardships they might have to face? Suppose—a larger fear—that she should fail to escape her accepted doom? Would he have the heart to remain alive in an empty world? Since her proposal had been made, the idea of such solitude had become hard to endure. He said, with sincerity in his voice, "I am not yet of a final mind."

CHAPTER ELEVEN

Wyndham left the council feeling that, if he had no special cause for satisfaction, yet that it had gone as well as, in reason, he could have hoped, and better than he had had some occasion to fear.

He had heard the second resolution—that for the sterilization of the seas—passed with the same unanimity as the first, he being excused from voting upon it in the same way as before, but that had been after it was agreed that he should confer privately with Pilwin-C6P to discuss the possibility of assisting the project if, or when, he should finally resolve upon the folly of avoiding the common death. It was a pledge which bound him to little, and which he had not seen his way to avoid.

He had not looked at Vinetta, nor, he supposed, had she looked at him. It was a cause of satisfaction that she had been discreetly silent, and had voted for the two resolutions in a manner which had drawn no notice upon herself. So far, he supposed, there was not, in any human mind, suspicion of what they proposed to do.

So far, so good. But suppose her attitude had been no less than sincere? Suppose that, with further thought, she had seen the terrible folly of the escapade which she had impulsively proposed? He knew how his own body, unacquainted as it was with pain or discomfort of any kind, shrank from the anticipation of what might—what *certainly would*—be before it, if his resolution should persist. And his body, inexperienced in hardship though it might be, was controlled by an ego of more vigorous, more optimistic, more barbarous days, while she had no such driving force, no such alien vitality. Would it be wonderful if she should reconsider?

He forced his mind away from this self-torturing doubt to wonder what his experiences might have been in that far life of which he could now have no memory. Would he, he wondered, recall them, however faintly, if they should be recounted to him? Suppose he should ask Avanah-F3B to describe what life had been in the England of that distant day? Would it be vaguely familiar? Would it perhaps come back to him as, by some accident of associated ideas, one is reminded of a dream which otherwise the waking consciousness would never have known? More probably, and more to the present point, might not knowledge of the barbarisms through which he had actually lived until yesterday give him resolution and courage for those which must be his again in so short a time? Certainly, he would have a talk with Avanah-F3B.

But suppose—his mind swung back again to its previous doubt—suppose she had seen the wisdom of that which was the considered judgment of *everyone of five millions* except themselves? A flicker of rebellion, a stir of insurgent life, might be natural enough, if she were really that sixth, unintended child. But was it likely that it would endure? Women are traditionally more disposed, even than men, to walk in the trodden path. Well, she had said she would come to him. She must stand the test. He would remain where he was, and, should she fail, they would all go to a common grave; for he saw now, with a convincing clarity, the folly, the barrenness of a single protest A misery to himself, to end in wretched, abortive death—and a jest to the mocking gods.

So he resolved. And in the mood of the torturing doubt which may be worse than despair he remained till the evening meal appeared; and after that, for some time, in a deepening gloom, for she was not quick to come.

But she did so at last, with serene eyes, and such a smile bending her lips that he was led to contrast the memory of how she had appeared to him during the earlier days; for it was a smile which, till then, he had never seen. He did not know that her coming had brought the same light to his eyes, and that he smiled in response to her, as Colpeck-4XP had never been seen to do.

"I thought," he said, "you would never come!"

"You didn't doubt me?" she asked, a shadow of disappointment darkening her eyes. And then, before he could reply, with a deeper realization of what they were, "We have begun to live, you and I, even before they are quite dead!"

He had risen when she entered, leaving a meal which, having been taken more rapidly than the regulations required, was nearly done, but a tiny dish of some opalescent material suggestive at once of china and polished steel, still showed a little untouched pyramid of mottled-grey powder. She looked at it as she asked, "Are you going to swallow that?"

"Yes," he said, "why not?" He looked bewildered, and then his eyes changed to a more understanding surprise. "I had not thought—" he began, and stopped, seeing all that her question meant.

It was this powder which, taken regularly, secured the body from extreme sensations of any kind. It could be discommoded neither by heat nor cold (which might have exposed it to greater dangers had not all extremes of temperature been banished, and fire rarely seen until the last hour of life, unless it were at a volcano's mouth); and the severest pain would be reduced to a slight, persistent discomfort, such as would be a warning that the physician's visit should not be long delayed.

That might mean nothing worse than an increased dose of the easeful drug, and a process of painless repair, or, if the damage were pronounced to be beyond remedy, there would be the journey to the euthanasia furnace, the taking of increased quantities of mottled powder, and a gradual sliding down in a failing consciousness to the pleasant glow of a furnace they would not feel.

"We might save it," he said thoughtfully, "for a great need, at a later time."

"I thought of that," she answered, "and then not. I threw it away."

She spoke with a hardening of eyes and lips which he did not miss. Had he been familiar with that ancient, profound fable of evolution, he might have recalled how Eve had plucked the fruit from the tree of knowledge, and given it to a less resolute hand. But he saw her to be determined in what she did, and knew that, happen what might, he would not doubt her again.

Still, he was unsure of the wisdom of this. Surely, such a power, such a protection, might be held for a great need? And then he remembered something which he supposed that she did not know, and saw what its implications were.

"You were right," he said. "I will do the same."

"What shall you say to Pilwin-C6P?"

"I will let him talk. He may think I am not yet resolved."

"But you will not let him persuade you to doubt indeed?"

"No. Now that I know your mind is equally fixed, I have ended doubt. You have my word upon that."

"Which I know well that you would not break."

"Yes. You can trust that. But I have not been thinking so much of Pilwin-C6P as of talking with Avanah-F3B. He could tell me much of the time from which I came, and among the barbarities of which I found means to live."

"Yes, you might get some ideas from him. Have you thought how you can get me clear without making more trouble than we could meet?"

"I have had many ideas, but none good."

"So have I, but yours is the better brain."

She added confidently, "But there is time yet. We shall find a way."

CHAPTER TWELVE

A few minutes later, Wyndham went to see Avanah-F3B, who specialized in history. That was according to the rule that those of lower rank in each hundred should become expert in a single subject, while those above exercised their minds in more general ways.

By the same rule, Colpeck had a wide knowledge of many subjects, but without particularity in any, he being ranked as one of the better brains. That was the custom throughout the whole organization of the five million of living men. It did not, beyond a point mathematically trivial, require or imply the inferiority of the specialist, as those at the head of each hundred were (very slightly) inferior to those at the foot of the hundred next above them, and there was thus no absolute superiority, except in the hundred, to which Colpeck-4XP and Avanah-F3B both belonged. But the arrangement was doubtless based upon the theory that it is a less severe test of human capacity to at-tain proficiency in a single subject than to have a well-balanced perception of all.

Actually, the subject was one that gave its professor a breadth of vision superior to that of the majority of his companions, for it had become habitual to him to consider this quiet twilight of the humanity to which he belonged, not only absolutely of itself, for satisfaction or scorn, but relatively to those earlier, more tempestuous ages from which it came.

He was a man who had lived an eventless life of a hundred and sixty years, and who was now conscious of some weakening of bodily reactions which, while they had not reached the point of definite disease, had been sufficient to suggest to an indifferent mind that the time to seek a pleasant, dignified exit could not be far.

"I have come to you," Wyndham began, "because I know that you can tell me much of that twentieth century to which I vitally belong, concerning which I have a natural curiosity, and which may include matters with which it may be profitable for me to be acquainted, in view of the difficult life which I may be leading after this week."

"It is a request," Avanah-F3B replied, "which it will be a pleasure to grant"—and indeed, where in any age could a professor be found who would not be glad to talk on his own subject?)—"but I must tell you honestly, not merely that there is a limit to what I know, but that I understand even less. How can I hope to make clear that which is confusion to me?"

"Perhaps," Wyndham suggested, "there may be some hope in the fact that my ego will be native to what I heard."

"Well," Avanah-F3B replied, "we can hope that." But his words did not have a sanguine sound. "You have no memory of those days. Can you stir that which you have not got?" He added, "Perhaps it will be best for you to ask whatever questions are in your mind, and I will give what answers I can."

Wyndham agreed that that would be a good way. He began: "My first question must be, if it were truly such a barbarous and bloody time, how did the men of that day endure it to the end, as we, under more tolerable conditions, are unwilling to do? And, in particular, how could the brain that was once mine, knowing all that it must have done, advise its ego that it would be preferable to return there?"

"The answer to these questions," Avanah-F3B replied, "is not easy to give, and I am conscious of my incompetence for the attempt. But it may be observed, in the first place, and on the evidence of one of themselves whom we had here, and whom I questioned for several days, that a large number *did* destroy themselves, even by most painful and repulsive methods. You must also allow for the fact that the majority of the men of that time appear to have been more or less mad. The actual number which had been segregated for that reason by their fellow-citizens in Great Britain alone during the year concerning which enquiry was made amounted to about two hundred thousand, this being the element of the population whose insanity was too absolute to allow of their walking loose; and there are abundant separate evidences that this mental unsoundness was more widely distributed. It was a matter of degree only. In many cases the warders may have had a measure of mental health little superior to that of those whom it was their duty to guard."

"It has," Wyndham allowed, "a very probable sound, and would explain much. I know already, that they sacrificed the safety and most of the amenities of life—such as they then were!—to the pleasure which they derived from sitting in machines which moved them about."

"That was so. But in the course of my researches I have come recently upon an even more curious evidence.

They had at that period a large number of buildings which they called prisons, in which they segregated a substantial part of the population. These people were housed, clothed, fed, and even amused without being required to undertake any compensating labour, such as was normally necessary at that period. Most of them belonged to sections of the population which, when outside these walls, lived precarious lives, liable to extremes of hunger, cold, or overcrowding in tenements less sanitary than the prisons were. They could not enter or leave such places by their own decisions, but only by that of tribunals which were set up to consider the case of each applicant separately.

"It has an incredible sound, but the evidence appears to be conclusive, that it was regarded as a penalty to be taken into one of these hostels, and a privilege to be expelled from them to face the rain or wind of the outer street."

Wyndham asked, "Does your knowledge of subsequent history enable you to tell me whether those men of the twentieth century were struggling in an opposite direction, or had they already set out on the road which is ending here?"

"Perhaps it would be the best guess that the evidence supports to say that they stood where the ways parted, and were uncertain which they would take. They acted, in consequence, as one of their own quadrupeds might have done had it been controlled by a rider who pulled it back from either road in turn, so that it reared and plunged, as the reins jerked and swung it, now left, now right, indicating each course in turn, and then refusing to let it go."

"I have no doubt," Wyndham replied, "that you are right. The men of that time may have been mad, and those of this may be saner than they. Or perhaps you may intend me to understand that insanity, which commenced at that day, has now come to the point which it was natural for it to reach. But, in fact—as perhaps," he admitted courteously, "I might have made plainer before—this was not the point on which I was most anxious to benefit from the special knowledge you have.

"I sought rather to improve my knowledge of the rough and perilous manners of life, such as may have approximated to what my own experiences are likely to be when this week is done."

"Then perhaps," the historian replied, "we may talk again at another time, when I may tell you things which will turn your mind from such an idea as that you can exist tolerably after your fellows have left the earth; if you have ever really had such a thought, which is very difficult to believe."

CHAPTER THIRTEEN

The chairman of the Council of the First Hundred (Munzo-D7D by name) had a great though placid pride in the place he held, and a special satisfaction now, that he should have such a position at a time of the culminating and concluding act of the race of which he was the intellectual head.

His fine mind was now exercised continually, and not the less acutely because it was without the stir of a hastened pulse, upon the coming consummation of human destiny, which he was resolved should be guided to its resolved end without fluke or blunder, and in a dignified manner.

In this connection he naturally gave prolonged thought to the case of Colpeck-4XP, which had developed in so unexpected a manner, and though the fact that it was no more than a barbarous ego that would survive tended to reduce both its intrinsic importance and its ulterior significances, he was not disposed to dismiss it from consideration without exhaustive examinations.

The facts that the race could not be continued by one individual, and that all their discoveries, their surgical devices, and cunning drugs, had taken them but a short step upon the path of enduring life, while they would rob the survival of anything more than residual importance, also made the decision of Colpeck-4XP more difficult to understand, and therefore to be examined with the more sceptical care.

So exhaustively did his mind penetrate the possibilities of the position that he even considered whether there might be any ape-like creatures existing in some remote, secluded part of the earth, from which a semi-human race could be born anew; and though he dismissed the possibility after sufficient enquiry, the idea that Colpeck-4XP must have some plan hidden in a lawless mind, such as would make mockery of that which his fellows did, still remained. Suppose, he thought, he were planning to save, at the last moment, some wretched woman against her will?

This occurred to him at once as being the most probable explanation, and the most dangerous possibility. It roused him to visit Avanah-F3B immediately that he heard that Wyndham had been talking with him; and learning little from the report of that conversation, which was readily given, he went on to consult Pilwin-C6P.

Avanah-F3B had said cautiously, "He had, as I think, doubts. His intention stands; but he is, as yet, less than firmly resolved."

Munzo-D7D felt even that hesitant intention difficult to believe without more explanation than he yet had, but he found that Pilwin-C6P could say even less, Colpeck-4XP not having yet made the promised call upon him. But he was willing to talk, and he took the question less impersonally than Avanah-F3B.

In fact, he asked bluntly, "If you have such a doubt, should he not be put to a quick end?"

Munzo-D7D shook his head gravely at this suggestion. "He has done no wrong. He has had permission to live."

"Which, if he thinks to be left alone, it is sure that he will not choose."

"So he may decide of himself. That would be the better way, and would end all doubt."

Pilwin-C6P did not dispute that, nor did he repeat his lawless idea that a man should be put to death who had not committed a legal offence, for he perceived it to be one which Munzo-D7D would not approve. But he thought—with which it is possible to agree—that men need not be over-careful of laws which are to end with themselves in the next week. Yet the tyrannies of convention and common order are very strong, and with these people they had acquired an almost irresistible power, so that he remained still, and Munzo-D7D went on:

"We are not discussing a likely danger, for it is most improbable that any woman would be willing to consider so intolerable a condition of life, and there has been no sign of such a tendency in any of those who, being in our own Hundred, are known to him: and if his purpose be to take one away with him against her will in the last hour—well, it would not be easy to do, and we can make it beyond his power."

"We could make a special law for a special case," Pilwin-C6P suggested, putting forward his first idea in a different dress, and with more wit than before.

Munzo-D7D considered this. It was not an unreasonable suggestion in itself, there being precedent for resolutions that one or more should die for the common good. But he saw that there would be a paradoxical absurdity here. They had given the man permission to live as long as he could, and would execute him at once lest he should abuse the license which they had allowed.

He saw that it was a proposal to rescind rather than pass a law. And he knew that there was an inertia of mind which made the men of his time reluctant to reconsider any decision to which they had deliberately come. If he were to propose it with any prospect that it would receive the necessary support, there must be, at least, some evidence, however slight, to explain his fear. He said, "Well, he will be coming to talk to you. You will judge his words with a fine care."

Pilwin was quite willing to undertake that. He added the best suggestion he had yet made: "You could ask him to pledge his faith in a formal way."

Munzo replied thoughtfully. "Yes. We could do that."

He went out through the wall of the apartment, which was violet shot with a dull red, and a moment later Wyndham Smith entered, as might be done without ceremony, it not being a private time.

It was only a few hours since, at Vinetta's prompting, he had rejected the daily potion of the drug which it was the universal habit to take, but already he felt a difference which had been puzzling to himself till he guessed its cause.

He felt more alive, more alert both to ill and good, more aloof from those among whom he moved, more independent of mind. It was as though he watched a moving pageant he did not share.

He took the visitor's seat, and Pilwin-C6P took that which custom allocated to him.

"I have come to discuss what help, if any, I might be able to give to your plans, if I should continue to live, as I may not yet have decided to do."

He was conscious as he said this that his voice had become somewhat brisker, more decisive in tone than he was accustomed either to use or hear, and he reminded himself that he must be cautious not to expose the difference which he felt. He might succeed in that. His greater danger was that he might come to underestimate the quality of the drug-ridden intellects against which he was obliged to contend.

Already Pilwin-C6P had noticed the change of manner. He looked slightly puzzled, faintly resentful, which meant much among this people of tepid emotion and measured thought. He answered, "I have given it some consideration, and I am not sure that there is much you could do, even with a better will than I believe that you have."

"Why should you think that? It was my own proposal that you should have the opportunity of realizing your ancestor's plan.

The retort, which came from the new freedom which Wyndham felt, seemed to him to have a convincing quality. As a debating point it may have been all he thought. The long moment of silence with which it was met seemed to give it his own value. But in the end Pilwin-C6P said only, "Well, so I think."

Wyndham could not get much change out of that. He reverted to that which he had been glad to hear, and which had sounded as though this matter might be disposed of more easily than he had feared. "Will you tell me," he asked, "why you think that I should be of so little use?"

"Because you have not the knowledge of the machines which the occasion requires. And even if you had, their control would be beyond the capacity of a single man, the major concentrations being so widely apart. You may ask why should not the success of one only be assured, if all cannot, but the problem is less simple. An error in instruction to one might destroy all in the next hour, for, though they are separate, their effects are interdependent in vital matters."

"Then it will be best for me to leave them alone?"

"There are some things you might do, if you have a good will, and can give your time for the next three or four days to mastering the rudiments of control, but I do not say they are much."

"Would they be beneficial to myself in the coming days?"

"No. Nothing would, as I suppose. You have made an impossible choice, unless you are friendly to dirt and pain."

"There may be even worse things."

"So there may. But that would be a poor reason for choosing them. The fact is," Pilwin-C6P went on, following his own thought, "it would be useless to attempt to continue control of the machines unless from twenty to thirty men should be left alive to give them the full guidance that they require. Short of that, it may be best to set them on a routine path, and leave them to their own ways, which may continue a long time.

"It might have been a good plan to leave that number, if they would have been willing to sacrifice themselves, or indeed, we might have resolved that the women only should go to a present death which would have been to make sure end of the race, while dealing with such matters as this in a leisured way."

Wyndham saw that this was true, but it was an unwelcome suggestion. Suppose it should be adopted at this late hour, even in a modified form, the hope of saving Vinetta would become even less than it now was. But he was sufficiently wary not to disclose his fear. He said, "So, no doubt, it would be. But men will not change a plan to which all have agreed, without more reason than that."

Pilwin did not dispute this. The talk turned to the conditions which would have to be faced on the earth by one man who would be alone, and with the machines either stopped or diverted from their present services. It was a subject on which the engineer had no useful suggestions to make, and his opinions were not pleasant to hear. "You may find food of a kind," he allowed, "though I suppose it will make you ill. But in a week you will be alive—if you still are—in a howling hell. Why do you not come with us in a decent manner?"

"Well, perhaps I shall. I may not yet be of a fixed resolve."

With those words they parted. Wyndham went, well content that the question of the machines had been put aside. For he had said definitely that he would not spend the rest of the week in acquiring knowledge of such doubtful value to the plans of Pilwin-C6P, and of less to him, and it was a decision which he had not been pressed to change. He thought also that he had suggested more doubt as to what his own decision would be than, in fact, he had.

Actually, Pilwin-C6P had been most impressed by a change of tone and manner which he had attributed to a wrong cause. "It is the savage ego that is exposing itself," he thought, "more nakedly as the hours pass. I suppose he will elect to live as long as he can, his instincts lacking reason's control. Well, let him go to death by his own road! It is nothing to us."

He repeated this conversation to Munzo-D7D, who gave it more thought, and whose conclusions were not entirely the same as his.

CHAPTER FOURTEEN

The next two days passed in ways that were momentous enough for some, including those of the processions that passed into five thousand furnaces of euthanasia, which, at the hour when the Council of the First Hundred met on the second day, were roaring hospitable reception to the fourth half-million reduction of the total of human lives, but to Wyndham and Vinetta they brought no change, except in themselves, though that might have been enough to engage their minds at a less critical time.

Wyndham had had two further talks with Avanah-F3B, and had added many more or less accurate facts to his previous knowledge of twentieth-century life, but they had increased his previous confusion rather than helped to elucidate the conditions from which his ego came, or supplied useful suggestions for the conduct of those which he was so near to experiencing. The facts might be comprehensible in themselves. Some of them were. But they would not coordinate. Each of them appeared to be contradicted or ridiculed by some other which was supported by historical evidence of an equal weight.

Discussing these difficulties with Vinetta, whom he continued to meet to the last limits of the hours which custom protected from observation, it had occurred to both of them that the explanation might lie in the difference which must divide a drugged from an undrugged world. They were already conscious of so much change in themselves, since they had ceased to use the mottled powder, that it seemed difficult to set a limit to its potentialities of explanation; but when Wyndham put this idea to the historian, he found that he had only increased the nightmare of improbabilities which he sought to probe.

He did not venture to mention that he had already commenced experience of a body from which the effects of stupefying and drowsing drugs were clearing away, for he had become too conscious of the vague suspicion with which he was regarded by his companions to disclose a deviation from that which was universal custom, and might be held to be compulsory law, so that he was debarred from making allusion to the resulting differences as he already knew them to be. But he suggested in general terms, "May not the absence of drugs of sufficient potency to control the actions and emotions of man account for the wild irregularities by which they destroyed each other's comfort, often sacrificing the lives they professed to value, or even undermining the health which they could only risk at such fantastic costs of humiliation and pain?"

"That," the historian replied, "like other suggestions which you have made, has a reasonable sound, nor can I say with entire assurance that it is less than true; but, in fact, the men of that time were takers of drugs to great amount, and in a variety by which it seemed that everyone should have been able to suit himself.

"There was one which they called alcohol, of a most potent kind, which was almost universally swallowed in the country from which you came. Its effects were admittedly bad, and their medical journals, while still advocating its use, commonly mention it as a principal cause of disease, insanity, and premature death, as well as being an incentive to violent crime."

"And you say that they still advocated its use? It has an incredible sound."

"They contended that it was harmless if taken in regular, limited quantities; or that it was actually beneficial as giving an illusion of geniality to the intolerable conditions of the existence which they endured."

"But surely the correct dosage could have been ascertained?"

"So it must appear. But you will remember the disorders, both mental and physical, of a time when, as I have told you, men would escape, if they could, from a safe jail!

"Neither does it appear that, though this drug had been used for many centuries by countless millions of men, they had been able to arrive at any agreed opinion upon it. Some held that it was detrimental in any quantity, at any time; while most, as I have said, contended that it was beneficial if not taken in excessive quantities.

"But you must not suppose that the men of that time depended upon this alone. They took drugs far more largely than we, and with intentions alike to ours. The difference was in the variety of these, and in the clumsiness of what they did. Occasionally it appears that a law would intervene to restrain those who were addicted to one of a particularly poisonous kind. But even in these cases there efforts appear to have been too weak, the penalties too mild; for the evils are mentioned as going on side by side with the preventive legislation, as two men might lie in one bed (as, on occasion, they did!). And of a thousand other drugs which the whole nation swallowed constantly, in pills and draughts, there was little knowledge and no restraint. You may say that the human race at that time was drugged continually, though without coherent purpose, or any unity of practice or of result."

"Well," Wyndham concluded, in a despair which may be simple to understand, "it was my own time, and I would believe of it the best I can. But you have called it mad, and I do not see how you can get beyond that. It may be that this drugging supplies the explanation of what they were."

"Even that," Avanah-F3B replied patiently, "might not be safe to conclude. It appears that some of the wildest words were spoken, some of the most sinister actions performed, by the more abstemious men. It may be best to say that they were maddened by misery and disease, by their perpetual motion and frequent wars, and put attempt at further explanation aside. But," he concluded kindly, "I need not say that our chemists would provide either alcohol, or any other of the drugs which their physicians prescribed, or which were used with less authority but even more generally, if you would like to be provided with them for the adventure you have in mind."

Wyndham shook his head. "My troubles," he said, "may not be so few that I shall need more."

"I should say that it is wisely resolved, But, if you will take counsel from one who can have been of little assistance to you in other ways, you will apply for your share of our own powder in its euthanasia form to be reserved for your use, and keep it closely at hand, for, I suppose, a few hours of a lonely life will be the most that you will endure."

"It will be mere prudence," Wyndham agreed. But he did not speak from the heart. It was only what he thought it to be mere prudence to say. For in the last two days he had come to love life as he had not supposed that he ever could, and to regard death with an equal fear, so that he would have said that it was more dreadful than pain, which he knew that Avanah-F3B, broad of mind though he was, would not find it easy to understand. Only if he should fail to rescue Vinetta might he be disposed to consider death as a fearful friend, and that would be in no mood of resignation, but sheer despair. All which might be thought, but must not be said.

So he went, feeling, as he had done before, that he had learned little which it could be useful to know; and that the lack of sympathy that was evident in those around him isolated him, even before the appointed day. Even the more vivid sense of living which had come with the abandoning of that mottled-grey powder did not incline him at the moment to more than a passive inclination to wait the event—or rather to concentrate upon the saving of Vinetta's life, and defer consideration of what must follow until they could breathe more freely in an empty world. He was waiting, with an impatience he must not show, for the rest of his kind to die. And so in this mood he came to take his place at the council table, to hear an event of the earlier day which stirred such emotion as he had not expected that his companions would ever show; and to learn that there could be an occurrence which would seem more dreadful, even more exciting, to themselves than it did to him.

It has been briefly mentioned already that the population of the earth, which had now been maintained for a prolonged period at a steady maximum of five millions, was settled in five thousand widely distributed centres, each consisting of ten separate mansions designed for the accommodation of one hundred inhabitants. Grouped with each of these centres were the technical buildings, museums, and libraries suitable to the tepid interests or activities of its population, the schools and nurseries which stirred into periodic activities, and, not least, the furnaces to which, one by one, at an average rate about six a year in each centre (but rising at some periods to a much higher level, owing to the fact that each quarter the population would be of approximately the same age) the older members of the community willingly went.

Originally there had been very beautiful gardens attached to these centres, but these, with one arbitrary and other necessary exceptions, had been destroyed as being too difficult to restrain within the standards of repression which policy and public opinion required.

The candidate for euthanasia would first partake of a pleasant meal, in which so large a portion of the daily drug would have been included, and of so potent a strength, that, as it penetrated his body, sensitiveness to pain, even in its severest form, would gradually cease, and a delicious, increasing languor would supervene.

Having partaken of this meal, he would enter the only place, in most settlements, where horticulture was still practiced—a hot-house of tropic flowers with overpowering odours, such as would drug the senses to pleasant dreams, even before the powder had had time to assert its power.

Here he would mount a couch, which would commence to move slowly, on smoothly grooved wheels, at a pace which he could either accelerate or retard, but which, if he should not interfere, would take him almost imperceptibly forward through corridors of increasing heat, which, as the drug worked, and he became more impervious, he would be unable to feel, until he would enter an antechamber of glowing metal, where he could watch the purple garment he wore catch fire, and wrap him in splendid flame.

Feeling no pain, though he might be aware of the scent of his roasting flesh, he could now, if consciousness still remained, touch the lever which would shoot him forward into the final furnace, where disintegration would be instantaneous, or he could continue to glide gently forward to meet his end.

It had been customary to keep these furnaces and their subordinate apparatus in constant readiness, so that there should be no risk that any applicants might be delayed who should resort to them at urgent need, but their actual use, averaging, as has been said, about once in eight weeks, had never risen beyond one or two daily, though their working capacity was much greater.

Now, however, they were required to provide accommodation beyond precedent, or anything which their designers had foreseen. At their maximum activity it had been calculated that it would be possible to deal with the present plethora of candidates at a rate of ten to the hour, thus allowing a two-hour interval between the semidiurnal batches, which was utilized for the inspection and renovation of machinery and apparatus which were not subjected to so unprecedented a strain.

On the first day the reports from all centres had been satisfactory to the most critical requirements. A million men and women had been eliminated without fault of organization, or any instance of unseemly hesitation or foolish haste. And so—apart from one solitary incident—it had been on this second day. But that incident had been of an appalling character. At Station 78F, situated where the city of Lubeck had stood in a more barbarous age, a hundred candidates, composed mainly of young women, with a few older men such as were non-essential to the concluding duties of the community, had been allocated to the third release, and were passing inward at the appointed intervals, when it was observed through the transparent heatproof walls of the antechamber to the final furnace that a young woman, Sinto-T9R, was showing signs of extreme perturbation at a time when she should have been reclining in languorous ecstasy, to the encouragement of those who watched, and who would go to the same fate in the following hours.

Perturbation, in the next minute, became panic fear. Her face became contorted with pain. She stopped her couch, and then drove it forward suddenly, having possibly intended a contrary motion and become confused by her condition. As she shot forward into a fiercer heat, her garment burst into flames. Her couch remained stationary for some long moments while she screamed and writhed and roasted in the sight of scores of appalled and impotent spectators. Then, freed from her own control, it moved forward again at its leisurely routine speed, and vanished into the white core of the ultimate furnace, from which, in due course, the metal frame would emerge, ice-cooled, and ready to be furnished anew.

The sight or hearing of this fearful agony had no effect upon those who were immediately following Sinto-T9R on the road to death, for her torment was not shared by them, nor, in their half-delirious, half-stupefied condition, did they show consciousness of what occurred. But to those who were destined to go the same way in later batches, and who had seen this disastrous sight, it was a different matter, as it was in five thousand centres when the incident had been broadcast throughout the world.

To the men of any age, it would be a disconcerting possibility that, where they sought euthanasia, they might encounter appalling anguish: but to these people, dreading pain as beyond endurance and outside the ordinary experiences of life, the possibility brought a horror not easily to be realized by earlier generations of men. The question of what had occurred, of responsibility for it, and most particularly whether it might occur again, stirred the world to a stronger ripple of life than it had experienced during the last fifty of its aimless, negative years.

The complement of the voluntary victims at Station 78F had been made up, it is true; but only after arrangements had been made for the instant reversal of the moving belt at the slightest sign of disquiet on the part of those who were approaching the final heat, and by calling for volunteers among those who had been intended for the immolations of later days.

It was one instance only of evident anguish, where there had been one and a half million painless deaths, but it had already caused a wild excitement sufficient to threaten the orderly termination of this supreme gesture of mankind's rejection of the rule of a blundering Heaven; and this confusion might increase during the next twelve hours, as volunteers must be found, or persuasions urged, to make up the quotas which the night required.

An authoritative decision as to the cause of the incident, and an assurance that it would not recur, had become of the utmost urgency; and the First Hundred assembled with faces at once graver and more alive than Wyndham Smith's adopted memory could equally recall. With his own mind released to increased alertness through freedom from the accustomed drugging, he regarded this unforeseeable development with satisfaction, as diverting attention from himself, but with a wary watchfulness for any threat to his own plans, or opportunity which it might bring.

But he saw that, for the moment, watching was all that he could do. He was the one man whom the event did not concern, who would not be considered to have the remotest interest in it. It was unlikely that his opinion would be asked. To tender it would be a gaucherie to which even his militant ego would not easily drive the settled habits of Colpeck-4XP. The chairman was speaking now.

"I am glad to say," he began, with the slow gravity of one who knew that he spoke to a waiting world, "that, only a few minutes ago, the cause of this tragic accident has been ascertained. It is an additional pleasure to be able to add that there is no reason to fear that it may happen again, nor to blame anyone who is alive for the blunder which has occurred.

"The necessity for producing exceptional quantities of the drug for which the occasion calls has resulted in a number of machines which were engaged in occupations for which they are no longer required being diverted to this purpose. Among these was one which had been designed for the manufacture of synthetic bacteria, by which it had been intended to supersede the uncleanly ferments which have been unnecessary hitherto for the fertilization of field and garden soils. This machine, though of exceptional intelligence and adaptability, has been found capable of error, and that error it is certain, by the result, that it did, in fact, on one occasion among three hundred and six, commit.

"The use of this machine for this purpose was authorized by Marceau-Z6B, who passed out of existence during the early hours of the present day. Orders, which I am sure you will approve, have been already issued for the destruction both of the delinquent machine, and for the whole of its products that remain unused. It has been ascertained that the use of this machine was no more than a needless precaution, the regular sources of supply, which are beyond suspicion, having proved themselves to be adequate to all requirements.

"The tragic horror which ended the existence of Sinto-T9R, terrible as it was, may be regarded as a demonstration of the basic equity of our protest against a form of sentient existence which is not divinely protected from such possibilities, and a justification of the course on which we are now agreed."

As he ceased, the sense of an enormous relief and of profound agreement with what he said caused a low murmur of approval to pass round an assembly which was little addicted to such demonstrations; and after that there was a long pause of silence, which was not broken until the chairman spoke again. "After this explanation," he said, "there can be little reason to doubt that the orderly procession which has faltered in the last hours will be resumed with the exactness which the occasion requires; but lest there should be any in whom a spirit of fear persists, it may be well that there should be some example among ourselves.

"We must, of necessity, be among the last to seek the peace that oblivion gives, having the direction of all. But that responsibility is not equally on the shoulders of every one. I propose that ten of us, five men and five women, shall volunteer to join the next hundred from this centre, and so go to immediate death. And lest it should be said that those who might volunteer might be of more courage than others, I will not leave it to your own voices, ready though I know you would be, but I will name ten, with the assurance that they will not be backward for the example which is required."

In an expressionless silence, as of an assembly that had now reverted to the trivialities of routine, he mentioned ten names, and that of Vinetta was second.

CHAPTER FIFTEEN

Wyndham saw the danger before Vinetta's name was mentioned, and in sufficient time to control himself to the expressionless calm that the occasion required. For what concern should it be to him?

He even had a premonition, approximating to certainty, of that which he was about to hear. Was it a trap, or no more than an evil chance? And what attitude would Vinetta adopt? What ground of refusal could she advance which would not concentrate suspicion upon herself? Or, if she should consent, what remotest hope of escape, of, evasion, could still remain?

Wyndham looked at her in an idle way, as, hearing her named, was natural enough, and was glad to see that she hid her thoughts, beyond what he would have supposed her able to do. Perhaps she also had guessed correctly what she would hear before the list had begun.

There was no haste to comment upon the proposal, which was received with the same silent, listless gravity by the nine whom, with Vinetta, it most concerned, as by the general body of the assembly. Tomorrow—or three days hence—could it matter much? It appeared to Wyndham that his companions had sunk into more than normal torpidity, as though in reaction from the excitement which had stirred them before.

But the Arabian on his right hand, seeing that no voices came from the lower seats, said, with the infinite weariness in his voice which made objection sound as colourless as assent, "It is unimportant. Let them go, if they will, as I do not doubt that they will be most ready to do. But I am not sure that it is wise. Would it not have been better to regard the incident as so fully explained, so entirely closed, that the resumption of routine might be assumed, and that no example was required?"

Wyndham, still too cautious to speak, heard this with a motion of hope which he must not show.

Vinetta lifted her eyes in a listless way. with a doubtful wisdom—but could she disregard this flicker of objection, which might die if it were not fanned to a wider flame?— she stated, "That was my own thought, but I would not speak it, lest it be misunderstood."

The voice of one near her offered hope of another kind. "Even though they volunteer, it must come to nought, unless there be ten from the routine list who will yield their places to them. Should we assume that?"

Slowly, one by one, others spoke to the same effect. Vinetta saw that the proposal would be put aside without further intervention from her. It was a danger narrowly missed; but was it as casual as it had appeared? She wished that she could be surer of that.

She heard the chairman withdraw adroitly from a position which was so plainly unsupported. He said, "There is much wisdom in what I hear. And, beyond that, the fact that the ten I named would have been willing to volunteer, as their silence told, is an example of as much force as though it had been done. As for the trouble of Sinto-T9R, it is over now. It is not a thing that would happen twice. Let all men put it from mind, and think only that they are near to the pleasant end of a weary day."

After that the council turned its attention to other matters, to which neither Wyndham nor Vinetta gave heed, waiting only till the time should come when they would meet, and could discuss what had occurred.

This they did when the hour of solitude came, Vinetta going to Wyndham's room, as it was her turn to do, at the first moment that prudence allowed. She commenced at once upon the peril through which she had passed, and with a force and freedom of expression which would have—sounded strange in her own ears a few days before.

"The old scoundrel," she said, "was aiming at me! I was sure of that. I could see that he was more savage to take it back than he would have been had he put it forward with no more purpose than he professed."

"I cannot say that I noticed that. Munzo-D7D is always expert to conceal his thoughts."

"So that little will mean much! Well, if you didn't, I did. I saw that he was hunting me from the first moment he spoke."

"Then was it prudent to interpose as you did?"

"Perhaps not. But it was a greater risk to keep still. I could not tell then how the others felt. The objection might have died out, and where should we have been then?"

"Not much worse than we are now, if he really suspects."

"You don't agree that he does?"

"Yes. I'm afraid I do, more or less. I doubt whether he would have made the proposal without more motive than he explained; and the fact that others thought it needless supports that probability, for it is a fact that his is the best brain in the world today."

"I will question even that, if it disappear by the week's end, and we contrive to remain; but I am not thinking that it will be easy for us to do."

"It is a hard chance, at the best; but it becomes desperate if he have a suspicion of what we plan. It is to fight the world, with all its machines, and its remaining millions of men. For, though he have no more than a small doubt, he will make certain you do not live."

He paced the room as he spoke with a restlessness that he could not still. Apart from this doubt, they had come no nearer to any plan than nebulous projects of flight or violence, or a combination of the two, to be undertaken when her time should arrive, at which moment they hoped that there would not be more than fifty men and women left in the world, which was a large place, giving many choices of secluded retreat, even with its surface stripped and levelled and tamed as it then was.

It was a difficult—indeed, an impossible—problem to guess what that remaining fifty—the best brains in the world—would do, when they should find rebellion just when they would suppose that the last hours of mankind had arrived, and they had composed their own minds to renounce the burden of life.

Would they still pass out in the same way, letting the dream of the extinction of the race go? It seemed too much to hope.

Would they endeavour to coerce by physical violence the woman whose rebellion would mock their plans? It was hard to imagine. Physical violences had become a legend of more barbarous days.

Suppose Wyndham should assault them with a lethal weapon contrived and secreted for the occasion? Would they resist? Would they go to death by way of a bloody scuffle, instead of the dignified, painless path they had designed? Imagination was baffled again.

Or, if they should observe Wyndham and Vinetta in sudden flight at the last hour, would they delay their own deaths for pursuit? Would they risk remaining alive, two or three score, in a world from which their customary amenities would be removed? A world of cold and heat and unfriendly winds, and of snow or rain that might fall in the daylight hours. It was still harder to think.

But Munzo-D7D might contrive to deal with it in other ways. He would be alive till the last, as his place required, as a captain must remain on a sinking deck. He was not to be despised, being bold and subtle and very wise. And he might still be able to control the machines.

Considering that, Wyndham had a doubt of whether he had not been foolish in refusing to spend these last days in obtaining knowledge of their control, as Pilwin-C6P had proposed. But it was useless to regret that. On the whole he could come to no better conclusion than that, if Munzo-D7D did not suspect, they had a most slender chance, but if he did, it was next to none.

So he said, in a mood of depression as strange to his previous experiences as were those of elation or self-confidence which he had known since the effects of the drug had cleared from his deadened nerves.

Vinetta, more elatedly conscious of a shadow which had nearly fallen upon her and now moved somewhat away, heard him in a frowning fear which she did not hide.

"You are not leaving hope?" she asked. "I thought you had been resolved that we should not lose! I think I should die if you fail me now."

She laughed shortly, in the next breath, at the literal truth of her last words, which she had not meant in that way, and, as she did so, their eyes met and the mood of doubt fell from him like a dropped cloak. She found herself caught in muscular arms that strained her close as their lips met. Then he said, "We will live, though the world fall. We will find a way."

"Yes," she agreed, made confident by her love, both in her own wit and the strength of those holding arms, "there is much that we must not lose! We will find a way."

Her words, confident as his own, yet waked him to sudden fear.

At the next moment they became alert to the fact that the hour of safety was done. There might be nothing in that. It was a small chance that she would be encountered in returning to her own room, which was not far. But her face paled as she became aware of the needless peril to which they had exposed themselves through that short failure of self-control. In a moment she was gone through the opaque, impalpable wall.

Next morning, having spent the night in devising resolute plans and subtleties by which suspicions might be turned aside, he went to Vinetta's room, to meet one who had been as sleepless as he, though she had spent the night in another mood. "I suppose," she said, "it is over now. I was seen to leave. You must let me die. Or, if we try it in the next hour, will it be less than useless to flee?"

CHAPTER SIXTEEN

"You will be safe," Wyndham said, "till the council meet, and even then we may turn suspicion aside by a bold, or perhaps by an indifferent front. Could you lie at sufficient need?"

She regarded him with grave eyes, to which some hope had returned, seeing how he had put the idea of abandoning her aside as not worth a word, and had equally refused to admit despair, or to consider immediate flight, which would have been to call the same thing by another word. "Yes," she replied. "I could do that."

It was not a question that would have been asked by the Colpeck-4XP of a week before. He had been of an exact integrity, both in act and word, which had been emphasized even at a time when disorders of speech or act were seldom seen in a placid life from which all forms of competition, all strong emotions, had been discarded, and irregularities of conduct were matters of speculative curiosity or tradition rather than experiences of living men.

But he felt differently now. He fought a battle of life and death, and the odds were millions to one. If others left him and Vinetta alone, so he would leave them. But if they threatened the life which was now of twofold responsibility and value, he would shield himself with whatever might most avail, be it truth or lie.

He had almost lost the feeling that he was one of a common stock, with the obligations that social order entails. The bond of allegiance weakened with every hour.

Apart from that, he had a feeling of responsibility for what had occurred. If he had not allowed love to seize the reins of his mind, to the exclusion of cooler thought, if he had not roused her for the moment, she would not have overstayed her time, and this danger would not have come to her door.

He did her the justice to remember that it was she who had shown the larger measure of self-control, that it was she who had broken away, who had remembered, although too late, the present peril in which they stood.

Blended with this, there was a feeling of fierce regret that they had made no more of a chance they had had—perhaps the last that they ever would.

They were alone again now, but their minds must be on different matters, in different moods.

Wondering half-consciously at himself, he proposed a plan, prompting her in what she should say to support the denial he had resolved, but he found it to be a matter on which she had no scruple at all. Loyalty and truth were as natural to her as to him, but they were to be given where they belonged. Chivalrous and abstract altruisms have always been the devisings of men rather than of those who must guard their young.

Vinetta said, "He will be slow to talk when he hears that." She approved a plan at once subtler and bolder than would have been likely to rise in her own mind. She added, "You had better go. We may not meet again till the last hour. But I understand. You can count on me."

They parted with few words, as having put emotion aside now the battle joined.

Wyndham went to his gymnasium exercises, which were a dead routine, as all was, now that competition had been condemned. These exercises were of a routine as exact and invariable as the meals, but took place in a common room. It was strange to observe men and women who would compass their own destructions on the next day, or before, exercising themselves lest their muscles stiffen or their digestions fail, but the force of custom was very strong, and what else was there to do?

Munzo-D7D entered the gymnasium. He looked round as one having an object in what he did. He saw Wyndham and crossed over to him. He said, "We must talk. Will you come to me when the hour of converse arrives, or shall I come to you?"

Wyndham looked at him carelessly. He said, "I have much to do. But you can come to me if you will. I suppose the talk will be soon done."

There was lack of customary courtesy here, though nothing at which Munzo-D7D could legitimately take offence. He said, "I will come." He went at that, having other matters with which to deal.

He came to Wyndham at the first moment he could. He knew enough to guess more, and his guess was good. He thought he could make a decisive end of the last trouble which humanity had to face as its twilight came.

There was no privacy in the conversation which followed, because anyone in the whole world who desired to do so could listen in. On the other hand it was an abstract improbability, apart from prior arrangement, that anyone would. Wyndham had no doubt that Vinetta would have tuned in to his own room of reception, which was why he had declined to visit Munzo-D7D, as courtesy had required. Otherwise than by her, he could not tell that he would be overheard, though he hoped he might.

Munzo-D7D knew that Pilwin-C6P and Avanah-F3B would be witness to every word that was said. He thought he had been wise to arrange that. It would have been wiser to have talked first in a more private way.

He began quietly, as was his natural manner. He did not think to make trouble, but rather to end it with a finality which he supposed that it would be easy to reach. He said, "The days pass. You have said that you have not been fully resolved, either to live or die. But it is a decision you cannot much longer defer."

"As to that," Wyndham replied, "I am now resolved. I have decided to live."

He saw that he must make provisions for continued existence which could not be concealed. Within a few hours, or a day at most, he must make his decision plain. Having one lie in his mind which must be stoutly sustained, he could not cumber himself with another of less evident use.

Munzo-D7D did not look surprised to hear that. It was, he believed, the truth, though he had not supposed that it would be so roundly declared. He went on, with a friendliness which he felt in a tepid way, though he knew it to be an alien ego to whom he spoke. "But do you think you are wise? You will be alone. You can have little comfort and less joy, but you will be sure of privations and many pains, for which your body is, by its training, unfit. And at last you must die in a futile way, and in a misery you can only dimly imagine, for it is certain that the furnaces will not endure. Is it worthwhile, for so certain and so unseemly an end?

He thought this question would lead to what he had come to say by a short path, but Wyndham's reply was unexpected, and delayed them both from the real issue to which they must come at last.

"Have you considered," he asked, "the old belief that we may be possessed of immortal spirits, and that what we do here may have consequences we cannot guess?"

Munzo-D7D looked with questioning surprise at the speaker of that which it was hard to take in a serious way; and jesting was an indecency which had long died from the mouths of men. He asked, "Will you tell me you believe that?"

"It is possible, and beyond disproof."

Munzo answered patiently, as one would bear with the incredible foolishness of a child. (Was it possible, he asked himself, that an alien ego could make no better use of a Colpeck brain?) "There are many grains of dust on the surface of the earth?"

"Yes, there are."

"There are countless millions even in a square yard of earth?"

"Yes. We agree there."

"If each of those specks of dust represented a million years, the aggregate would be beyond our power to conceive?"

"It would be very long."

"But to eternity it would be nothing, though it were multiplied a million million times, and by that again?"

"So, to our finite minds. it appears to be."

"So it is. Can you think of that, and imagine that all our futile human births will continue thus? It is not for wisdom to entertain."

"Yet, we are now. We may be then. Not understanding what reality is, we may refuse to assert, but must we not equally refuse to deny?"

Munzo, who had spoken so far with more quickness of reply than the habit was, reacting to the speedy answers that were given to him, became silent. He restrained himself from what he felt to be an irrelevant issue. He asked, "And you have no other reason than that?"

"Having given reason enough, need I add more?"

Munzo became silent again. He had brought the conversation to the point at which he must make a direct attack. "If," he said, "you had a hope which will prove false, it would be kindly to let you know?"

"I have little hope, so you need have no trouble for that."

"But if you had?"

"Even so, I do not ask you to interfere. A false hope is soon done, and there may be nothing better to take its place. But I suppose I have none. You choose your way, and I mine. You can let me be."

"But if you plan to have a companion, making a mistake in that?"

"Why should you invent that? I have told you it will be wiser to let me be, lest I say more than you would be willing to have publicly known."

Munzo considered this in a quiet pause, being a genuinely puzzled man. He said at last, "Your words have no meaning to me."

"That is how I feel about yours. I do not interfere with what you may plan to do. It is nothing to me. Why are you concerned about mine?"

"I will tell you in simple words. Vinetta has been to your private room at a monstrous hour. If she plots to live, it will come to nought. We shall make sure provision for that."

"Who has told you that foolish tale?"

"It is no tale. It is what I have seen with my own eyes."

"That is to say, you will assert that which is absurd in itself, and for which you have no confirmation at all. Vinetta was here, as we know, though it was not at a monstrous hour. It was later than that. And you can guess what she was here to say. But is all nothing to me. You can persuade her to what you will, or she can refuse. Being the man who is to remain alive at the last, you can do what you will, but I say again it is nothing to me. You must find another, if Vinetta prefer to die."

Munzo stared at this, as he well might. He said at last, "I do not know what you mean. You talk as though you are mad. But that is not my concern. I have warned you how it will be, in a friendly way, and you must live or die as you Will."

Wyndham answered, "As you say you have finished, you may now listen to me. Vinetta told me the offer you made to her, which she did not accept. If I wished your death, or regarded her, whether she live or die, I could tell the Council all that I know, and I suppose they would arrange your death on a sooner day. But if you think to protect yourself by a false tale, such as would convict Vinetta and me, I will tell the truth, and I suppose she will do the same, and you will have brought the trouble on your own head."

He rose as he spoke, which was a signal for his visitor to leave which no man could disregard. Munzo-D7D rose also. He said, "I had not thought that a barbarous ego could bring such wickedness to a disciplined brain. It is cunning beyond belief, which you will find useless to you."

Wyndham asked, "Are you sure you are not imputing yourself to me?"

Munzo went without attempting further retort. He walked like a man dazed. But Wyndham did not overlook that he had the best brains in the world, though they might be drugged to the pace of a sluggish blood. He thought that further trouble would not be slow to arrive.

CHAPTER SEVENTEEN

As he left Wyndham's room, Munzo-D7D thought more briskly than his habit was.

He did not doubt that Colpeck-4XP plotted to save a woman alive and so continue the race, making a mock of the five millions who were now going to death for what would be no more than an empty dream. He had suspected it, in advance of proof, and had correctly deduced, first that such a woman must be of his own thousand, and most probably one of the hundred of his own house, and then going over the two score or more of women that the First Hundred included, he had settled upon Vinetta as the one whom Colpeck-4XP would be most likely to choose, and who would be most likely to consent to join in so gross a crime.

He had seen in the event of yesterday an opportunity of eliminating this danger while pursuing a separate object, and he admitted frankly to himself that he had blundered in that. He saw also that to the extent to which he had kept his purpose in his own mind, these preliminary activities could be construed in a false way, and that it was a wickedness which Colpeck-4XP—so tragically, so fundamentally changed now!—would not scruple to commit.

He saw that he could conclusively refute accusations against himself by going the way of death at an earlier day, but he saw also that this would be to accept defeat on the major issue, which he was resolved that he would not do. Where he had, though, to enforce discipline in a dignified, emotionless way, he found himself involved in a struggle which threatened his own honour, the credence and confidence of his fellow-men, and the success of the great project in which they were cheerfully joined, against a boldly defiant and incredibly unscrupulous foe.

With these thoughts chaotic in a storm-tossed mind, he yet showed the quality and promptness of his judgment by resolving to go instantly to Vinetta, to challenge her with her offence, and to convict her, if he could, of the truth, or snare her to a different lie from that which her fellow-conspirator had told.

He delayed only to call on Pilwin-C6P, to ask him to listen in on the coming conversation, and to call up Avanah-F3B that he might do the same.

Pilwin-C6P was quite willing to do that. He was pleasantly excited by what he had heard already. He had even thought that, if such events as yesterday's and today's should become frequent, it might have been almost worthwhile to remain alive. That was in a world of continuing comforts, of course. No heat or hunger for him! He had too much sense.

"Yes," he agreed readily, "that is the best thing you can do. If you can get her to admit in our hearing that she has been plotting with Colpeck-4XP, you will have no more trouble with her. And if she be alive this time tomorrow, after admitting that, she will be a most clever girl. And, besides, you will have gone a long way towards clearing yourself."

That was not a view of the matter at which Munzo could take offence, though it was one that he did not like. He saw, with an increase of irritation, that it was logically sound. To prove that Vinetta had been plotting with Colpeck-4XP did not demonstrate that he had not approached her also with a proposal which he, as the man who was to be last alive, would be particularly able to make. Rather, it might be urged, his own rejected advances had put him on the track of his more favoured rival. It may be held to be an evidence of some courage, as well as of an integrity which there was never true occasion to doubt, that the idea of abandoning the investigation did not enter his mind.

He went on to Vinetta, who did not object to seeing him, but who looked at him with a smouldering hate in her eyes which she made no effort to hide.

"It is no use coming to me again," she said, before he had time to begin. "I have given you my last word, which I will not change."

"You have given me no word at all," he replied, seeing that he was to be met with a concerted tale, and striving to control himself to speak such words as it would be well for others to hear. "I have not spoken to you, outside the council room, for more weeks than I have leisure to count. Will you hear what I have to say now before you reply?"

"Yes," she said. "I will listen, though expect it will be to hear lies, such as that which you have just said."

"All men," he replied, with some dignity, "know that I do not lie."

"So they know of me, and more particularly of Colpeck-4XP; which is why for my own protection, I have confided in him. And, besides that, he is one who stands apart, by the decision that he has made, so that he can bear witness to all with impartial words."

"If you have the integrity that you boast," he replied, "will you go to death in the next batch? If you will do that, there is no occasion for further words."

"But why should I? So that the only witness against you may be removed, and you make proposals to some other girl which she may receive in a different way? No, indeed! You may accuse me of what you will. I will defend myself with my living lips. Why should I be afraid? I am of the First Council as well as you. It is you who should go to an early death, as I shall not scruple to say."

"You are the Unlawful Child," he said as though thinking aloud. "I suppose that will explain much. But I should not have thought that even the influence of the barbarous ego for whom you sin could have made you so cunning and bold to lie."

"It is you who lie. You do not even know that I am. But I suppose it was because you thought that, that you approached me with the proposals I would not hear."

"I will say no more," he replied, with a temperate restraint which it is possible to admire. "The whole matter shall be laid before the council tonight."

She found no satisfaction in hearing that. If he had not been frightened to silence by the accusations which had been suggested against him, the battle was still unfought, and the issue was hard to meet with a sanguine guess.

He left her, marvelling at the wickedness with which his zealous efforts for law and order had been defied. Surely such criminalities belonged only to the traditions of ancient days!

But so it was. Eve, who had plucked at the tree of knowledge before, now plucked at the tree of life with a sharper need, and sin had re-entered the world.

Munzo-D7D went on to Avanah-F3B, thinking to confide in him, and to get some comfort therefrom; for the historian was friendly, they having congeniality of disposition, and being accustomed to spend much time together in the conversations which, dull and slow as they might have sounded to the ears of another age, had become the most stimulating occupation of millions of wearied lives.

He was received with interest and the sympathy which he expected to meet. Curiously, Avanah-F3B, though harmless himself as an elderly sheep, seemed less surprised, and far less horrified, by what he heard than either the narrator or Pilwin-C6P had been.

Perhaps, as a historian, he was so familiar with plot and crime that the strangeness of such ancient depravity intruding into a civilized age did not impress his mind with the aspect of monstrosity which it showed to them. He was not shocked or incredulous. He was mildly interested, even mildly excited. It was like one of the ancient tales in the consideration of which his life consisted, rather than in its placid contemporary environment.

He even had a passing wish that he might live to know what would happen. Personally, he would not object, nor speak a word to hinder, if it should appear probable that Vinetta, or any other young woman, should survive to become the mother of a new race. The proposed exit of humanity from the records of time had a dramatic quality which had pleased his mind, and he had given it the support of a ready vote. But so also did that of the surreptitious survival of two who would renew their kind, so that a new vista of history would commence with the next dawn. He would regard that with equal benignity, tempered only by regret that it was something he would not see.

But, if the thought that he would no longer live brought a feeling of sorrowful regret, he did not therefore hesitate in his own intention. It would be pleasant to watch, but not at the cost of discomfort to his own skin. A man may love drama, but he will not wish to watch the play with a cold draught blowing about his legs.

He disconcerted Munzo-D7D, as the narrative closed, by saying with friendly sincerity, "If you have really such a purpose, and can find a woman more complaisant than Vinetta has proved, it will be an act of friendship to tell me more."

Munzo was confounded by this to a point at which his resolution to inform the council faltered. If Avanah took it thus, how might it appear to others who would regard it in a spirit less friendly and less detached?

He returned to Pilwin-C6P, hastening his steps more than was seemly for a man to do, for the hour of siesta was near, and he was determined to resolve the question of whether or not he were doubted by him also without further delay. Pilwin was amused. He had listened in, as he had, for a second time, been requested to do. He said, "You have touched fire with a bare hand. Whoever lies, there is no doubt that Vinetta thinks herself equal to dealing with you."

Munzo answered, "She may be equal to me or not. The question does not arise. She thinks herself equal to defy the council and put us all to contempt. That is a greater thing, which she must not do."

"Well," Pilwin said, as though it were a matter on which opinion should not be hastily formed, "be it truth or lie, you are one who should know best. But I will say this: if they lie, they lie well." He added, "The barbarian has asked to see me this afternoon."

"You have agreed?"

"Yes. I had intended to watch the furnace at work. I like the glow of the inner blaze as it is thrown on to the roof of the antechamber when the doors open. But I will see him. It is for your sake rather than mine. I will get the truth if I can. Or perhaps you will not thank me for that? Should I put it another way?"

Munzo asked, "Am I to suppose from that that they will fool all men with their incredible tale?"

"Not at all. They have not made me believe. But you must allow me a space in which to weigh all in an open mind, as reason prompts us to do. Especially as it is all the occupation I have. As to sterilizing the seas, I have given all the orders the occasion requires. But I can tell you that they will not succeed.

"I have had reports today of the conditions in the lonely parts of the earth where men have ceased to resort, and as for the suppression of life, it is evident that it cannot be done. Or I should rather say that concrete is the sole cure.

"You know how we have tried. The hunting machines, large and small, that make fuel from their prey, so that they do not cease to pursue, nor to fill their maws—the inoculations, the spreading oils, the dosing of great districts with extremes of heat and cold, such as most creatures cannot endure, the great electric shocks—they have done much, but the reports from all sides are that life is insurgent again in a hundred forms. We may make an end of ourselves, but it will remain a disease that we cannot cure."

Munzo listened to that which would have interested him more at another time. As he had observed Pilwin's reaction, and remembered that of his previous auditor, judgment warned him that the tale which Colpeck-4XP and Vinetta had conspired to tell might be sufficient to confuse counsel, even though it should not be confidently believed. Where he had not hesitated for his own repute, he paused at the thought of the larger issues which it was his duty to guard.

He said, with courtesy, "By your leave," he said in an act of rudeness, at which Pilwin must stare incredulous surprise. Then the explanation came. He reached to draw forth the writing materials of his host without permission for such a liberty being given. Having obtained them, he wrote, "I would not ask aloud, lest we be overheard. I would have none guess what I now do."

After that he drew swiftly and well. Their eyes met, and, more than once, Pilwin nodded assent. When he rose to go Pilwin had no doubt of his integrity, that they were led by one who would bring all to the resolved end. He settled himself to his midday rest with a satisfied and amused mind. It was a mental attitude which did not change as he thought of the visitor he was to receive during the afternoon.

CHAPTER EIGHTEEN

Wyndham came to Pilwin-C6P with intention both to conceal and deceive, and with the purpose of acquiring information it might be useful to have, and, perhaps, to gain active help. He had no inclination to give further trust because he was received with more cordiality than had expected to meet. He was wise in that Pilwin had reserves in his own mind, and if he gave help it might be such as leads to a covered pit. There were deceits in his heart such as it had not held till that hour, for when Eve reached for the fruit was to be more than a single sin; a life repeats itself in a round that is never different, though it is never the same.

Wyndham said, "I ask your help. I must choose a place where I will live when I am alone in the world. I know that you have special knowledge of what the climates were before we controlled the winds, which I suppose they will be again."

"Could you not go to the librarian for such information as that, rather than come to me?"

"I have been to him. But he knows so much that I am merely confused. He suggests a hundred places, and has objections to all."

"Well, so there are."

"I believe that. But I must make a choice."

"So you must, if you persist in this crazy attempt. I will tell you frankly what I think. Go where you will, you are not likely to endure for a moon's length. I should guess at ten days, if not less.

"You must consider that, though men lived when the winds were loose, they were born to tempest and frost and heat, while you have been bred in a different way."

"I have thought of that. That is why I desire an equable spot."

"Which will not be easy to find. But there is one thing in your favour. That is, if you stay in this Northern Hemisphere, as I suppose you intend to do, it is the time of the year when the light will increase, and the air will be more or less temperate, even at night, for three moons, if not more.

Wyndham knew that. He wished to get an answer to his first question. He asked again, "Well, where should you advise me to go?"

"It is not easy to answer. Will it be well to stay in one place? If you wander north for six months, and then south for the same time, you may think to avoid extremes, either of heat or cold, though you may find in practice that it is less simple than that. Primitive men did not generally do so, having houses and herds and young children, and other things which would have been awkward to move about. But you will be quite alone."

"Yes. It will be a greater loneliness than the earth has known."

"Well, it is your choice! So you might wander at will. But when I think of this, there is another difficulty which I can see. There is the question of food. You must grow, and, I suppose, store food. You will require archaic, primitive tools. Have you thought of that?"

"I have selected a number from our museum already."

"Well, you see what I mean. Even though you may be quite alone, you will have too much to carry about. Primitive people had domestic beasts of burden and perhaps carts. But there are none of these left in the world. You might have a machine. But would it last under your single control?"

"I will have no machines. They have wrecked the world."

"Well, if they have, they have. But what is it to you? You need not consider that. You are not founding a new race. But I see reason to doubt how long a machine sufficiently simple to control would be obedient to you. You may be wise to commence as you must go on."

"Then where should you advise me to be?"

"I have thought that a mountainous district may be best, in what was the temperate zone, and will doubtless be so again, As the seasons change, you can go up or down. You will find a great difference in climate can be reached in that way by no more than an uphill walk, or a short descent.

"I have thought whether you could move growing food in the same way, planting it in boxes, and drawing it up or down, but I doubt whether you will find it a satisfactory plan."

"No. I don't think I should. But what mountain do you recommend?"

"Well, you might find it best to choose one where we are growing trees, of which there are few. I believe that wood is required for many purposes in a primitive life. There is Mount Ida, in Asia Minor, where men lived, I believe, in remote times. You must not think that I recommend it. Go where you will, I suppose you will be a most miserable man. But I can think of nowhere better than that."

"Neither can I. It sounds to me a good choice." Wyndham recognized advice that seemed to be honestly given, and in itself sound. After some further talk, he said definitely that that was where he would go.

"You will gather what you require, and go tomorrow, I suppose, while the means of transit are still reliable."

"No. I have decided to wait the end. I will have the comforts of decent life for as many days as I can."

Pilwin did not argue about that, though he pointed out that the running of the long-distance automatic cars might be affected almost immediately by the changed conditions of the earth and the new uses to which its major plants would be put. "You might go safely," he said, "or you might end in a ghastly death, or be maimed in a disconcerting manner which you will wish to avoid."

But even on this matter he was helpful. Why should not one of the aeroplanes which were accustomed to cross the world with certain supplies such as were required while they were fresh be used for this final service?

"It is true," he said, "that they are not designed for human occupation, but you would have courage for that, and the question of skill would not arise, I could even procure you one which is accustomed to alight in the district to which you propose to go."

"It would be a service of kindness," Wyndham agreed, "for I could not go in a quicker or better way, and it will carry the tools and garments that I require."

"Well, I am glad to help you in so simple a matter. Considering that my own troubles are so nearly done, and the nature of that which, at the best, you will have to face, it is a small thing to assist you the best I can."

Wyndham thought that this sounded sincere, as it partly was. With repeated thanks, he would have risen to go, but Pilwin changed the subject abruptly. He said, "This is a queer business about Vinetta and Munzo-D7D. I should not have thought him one to design that which would be both folly and crime."

"You have heard something of that?"

"Yes. I listened in, at his own request, when he was talking to you.

"Well, when you call it crime, I suppose you are right. You cannot expect me to call it folly, except in thinking that Vinetta would agree. I suppose few women would."

"I should have supposed none. He must have placed his hope in her as the Lawless Child. I wonder how he thought to save her life when her turn came in the procession of death, she being nearly sixty before the last?"

"She didn't know. He told her no more than that he would provide her a way."

"Well so he would have done, I suppose, had she agreed. He has a fine brain. It was well that she had discretion to refuse, and to come to you. I wonder why she did that?"

"She may have thought that I should believe her tale better than most. But it is a question to be asked of her rather than me. As she refused, it can be put out of our minds. Why should we vex the thoughts of others before they die?"

"So I think. Would you have taken her yourself, if she had been willing to go?"

"Yes, I would. For two are better than one. But it is not a life to persuade any woman to share; and when I heard them all vote for their own deaths, I put such thoughts from my mind."

Wyndham went, and Pilwin pondered the conversation without coming; to any definite conclusion, though he wondered whether Vinetta had offered to go with Wyndham, and might still hope to do so.

"Well," he said to himself at last, "be it as it may, there will be provision for all."

CHAPTER NINETEEN

Wyndham went to the council prepared to meet whatever accusation might be made against himself and to support Vinetta in the tale which he had prompted her to tell. Doubtless she went in the same mood. But they found that they had armed themselves for a battle which did not come. Seeing that there was to be no open conflict, he watched narrowly for a flank attack—for some proposal which would make certain of Vinetta's death, without disclosing that as its direct purpose. He did not underrate the ability of the brain that was in opposition to his, nor the fact that it had the overwhelming advantage of being on the side of the universal decision, with all the material forces of civilization in its support.

He saw that, if such oblique attack should be made, it might be difficult for either Vinetta or himself to resist it without drawing suspicion upon themselves and perhaps leading to a position which would discredit them in advance, if Munzo-D7D should subsequently charge them with the conspiracy he had discovered. But he could do little even mentally to prepare for an attack the nature of which was so vague a conjecture. He was like a general who cannot tell from what quarter his foes will burst out of the fog that surrounds his lines. And, in the result, there was no attack at all. The meeting went on its quiet, leisurely course, already laden with the atmosphere of approaching peace and with the news from all centres that men and women slid punctually to their easy deaths.

And the next day passed in the same way, with its reduction of a further million of remaining lives, and Munzo-D7D still gave no sign. He had even abandoned his previous intention of asking Colpeck-4XP for a solemn pledge that he would not seduce a companion to share his renunciation of this final gesture by which mankind would reject their Creator's will. It had become too plain that the confidence he would have felt in his companion's veracity—he would have said in his honour—would be misplaced. The position must be dealt with—was being dealt with already—in other ways.

The day passed without Wyndham and Vinetta meeting except by casual, public chance, when they did not speak. They had both seen, without consultation, that the secret meal-time contacts must be abandoned. While there had been no suspicion directed upon themselves, the law-less audacity of the proceeding, joined to the fact that all men were in retirement at the same hour, had rendered it a matter of little hazard. But now, if any could be found who would shorten their own retirement for so great a cause, there would be no difficulty in stationing them in innocent, neutral positions, such as would enable them to observe the crossing from one room to another. And who would believe that they could engage in indecencies so profound with less motive than in fact they had?

They were long hours for Vinetta who must spend them in the customary indolent manner, but for Wyndham, making preparations which must appear to be for one only, so that many things which he would have collected for Vinetta he must not touch, they were soon gone.

In the early afternoon the aeroplane from Asia Minor arrived and settled with the seeming discrimination of an alighting bird, upon the landing-place to which it was drawn by its self-regulating magnetic controls; and he began to load it at once, finding a curiously exciting pleasure in a sense of ownership more particular and absolute than he had previously known. He knew it to be a barbarous atavistic instinct, but what thrill it gave of exultant con-quering life! And when he should add Vinetta—dearest acquisition of all—to the cargo he would bear away through the skies, he would have found life, which he saw that those around him had never had. That was why they were destroying themselves. They were not doing anything more than to recognize an existing fact.

He felt himself to be alone already, among the walking dead—more alone, far more than he would be when two dawns had come, for the dead kept him from the one other who was alive. In this mood he went too near to despising the sluggish brains and timid pain-dreading bodies of those among whom he moved. What power was theirs to contend with the undrugged brain of a living man? He moved with confident steps, feeling a disposition to sing, but having no words or tune for so primitive an exhibition.

In the afternoon the museum, from which most of his ancient treasures were taken, became vacant, and entirely at his own disposal. The curator, one of the fourth hundred and also a Colpeck (-4GZ), had been friendly, and given him much curious and possibly useful information respecting articles in his charge.

He had shown him replicas, ancient in themselves, of still more ancient things, among which had been weapons such as had been used in very barbarous times. Short broadswords, such as the savage Romans had used to stab upward under their enemies' hearts: long Polish lances of a later millennium, which had been the still more curious weapons of men who sat on the backs of animals more primitive than themselves.

Showing these, he had mentioned a tradition of those savage, quarrelsome days, that the nation which used the shorter weapon would always dominate those who tried to reach their foes at a longer range. Remembering this, Wyndham selected the Roman sword. He made himself grotesque to his own eyes by girding it to his side with a leather belt. He practised with it, cleaving a block of oak, till he observed that he had dulled its keenness of edge, and must labour awkwardly to sharpen it to his own satisfaction again. He did not show this weapon abroad, having a thought which he feared, probably without foundation, might arise also in other minds.

He spent some time also in apparent indolence, loitering round the furnace, and watching the process of dissolution to which the men and women he knew submitted themselves in a placidly contented, mildly excited, unbroken stream.

They did not object to his presence there. Rather it was a sight to reconcile any who might otherwise have felt a pang of reluctance, a disposition to regret the mystery of existence which they were casting away before the inevitable hour when it would have been taken from them. To think of the fearful life which would be the penalty of his unnatural rebellion against the universal verdict was enough to hasten them contentedly through the humid atmosphere and intoxicating odours of the conservatory toward the consuming heat of the central fire, which would be as pleasant to feel as it would be beautiful to see.

He even penetrated into the preliminary hothouses which his exceptional position enabled him to do without causing it to be supposed that he was seeking dissolution before his time. Idly he watched a crawling automaton passing from pot to pot, raising itself to drive a long sensitive proboscis into the soil of each, and then going off to communicate the information it had recorded to another automaton, which would subsequently give to each the water that it required. With equal indolence he lounged round the outside of the antechamber to the final portal, where others stood to watch the disappearance of friends into the irrevocably devouring flames.

It was next morning that he passed Vinetta, and said casually, "Do not object to enter the furnace when your time shall come. You will have nothing to fear."

It was unlikely that any would notice or overhear, but, if they should, what was there in that to raise objection or cause remark? The words were not spoken in a furtive or significant manner, and their substance was no other than excellent advice. Vinetta heard them with an instant's blankness of incomprehension, an instant of incredulity, of fear. But it was no longer than that. With a recovered serenity, she answered, "No, of course. I shall go when my turn comes! There will be nothing to fear."

After that, he appeared to take no further notice of her. But he watched in a constant dread. His fears fluctuated between the doubt that the aeroplane which had been suggested for his use might be the bait of some fatal trap, and the greater probability that Munzo-D7D, or perhaps Pil-win-C6P, of whom he had an almost equal distrust, might have devised something against Vinetta from which, as he could not guess it, he might fail to give her the protection that she required. Well, he must trust something to her. She was no fool. Her thoughts would move on the same lines as his own. And of her courage he had no doubt.

The latter was the more probable danger, both because he could imagine no possible way in which the aeroplane could involve him in any peril, though he exhausted his imagination upon it, and he did not think that the probity of Munzo-D7D—which he did not credit the less because of the criminality of his own mind—would allow him to practise against the life of one whom the council allowed to live, without obtaining formal revocation of that deci-sion. Vinetta was in a different position. To ensure her death was to enforce the popular will, which was also rati-fied by her own consent.

But the day came and went, and nothing sinister hap-pened at all. The last council was held. The last disposi-tions for the slackening control of the earth which men had shown themselves so incompetent to possess had been made. The night passed. The dawn rose which mankind had resolved should be the last it would ever see.

As it broadened across the sky, the last million of hu-manity began their procession toward the annihilation which they considered to be the final end of their separate lives. At Wyndham's centre the incineration of the Second Hundred commenced. That of the First Hundred was to follow immediately after the usual two-hour interval, for which, however, there would be no occasion at the other centres, at which the destruction of the penultimate would be followed immediately by that of the final Hundred. This arrangement was possible because the resources of the furnaces were sufficient for the last act without renewal or renovation of their resources, and was convenient because it allowed the council time for a brief final session, at which it could receive reports that the last Hundreds had entered upon the procession of death.

CHAPTER TWENTY

As it turned out, Pilwin-C6P was not actually late for the last council, but he would have been so in the next second, and he was the ninety-ninth to take his place, the hundredth seat remaining vacant, for Colpeck-4XP did not come.

There was little regard for that vacant seat. He who had renounced the decision of all his race might go his own way, as the time was obviously arriving for him to do. He had been seen until a few minutes before, hanging round the furnace with that absurd weapon swinging against his thigh, and what his fate would be in the coming days was not pleasant to think. It would have been easy to feel a gentle sorrow—the strongest emotion which a well-controlled human ego should be permitted to experience—for a man so enamoured of dirt and pain, had it not been neutralized by an equally faint contempt.

Munzo-D7D, looking down the two familiar rows, was more interested to observe that Vinetta's seat was filled. Her face showed the same placidity that was the common expression of those around her. A placidity beneath which there was a faint pleasure, a mild relief, as of those who have come through a boring day, but who know that the hour of repose is near.

Pilwin-C6P had delayed for a message to reach him from a distant station—HI4—which, when it came, would have had no meaning to any but him. His eyes met those of the chairman as he took his seat, and he gave a slight but sufficient nod. Munzo-D7D understood that the necessary dispositions had been made. Vinetta might go to her death in a seemly dignified way, such as would be painless for her. It might be supposed that she would. But if some evasion had been contrived, it would be the worse for her. Much the worse. There would be no difference beyond that.

Munzo-D7D put her out of his thoughts. He had a speech to make, and that was an occupation that gave him the greatest pleasure he had, which may not have been overmuch. He spoke the funeral oration of mankind, which, to mankind at least, was to deal with a momentous event.

But what he said was simple and short. The decision to which they had come, and which would be consummated and concluded before the next sun should rise, was not hurried, nor such as might have been altered had it been subject to longer debate. It was a decision to which mankind had been slowly tending, as Avanah-F3B would have told them, from the barbarous ages—from as far back as the twentieth century, when mankind had blasphemed and rejected the traditional God by telling Him flatly from a half-populated earth that a few children were much better than more.

What natural alternative was there? To beat vainly at doors which would never open to human cries? Or to go the way of endless futility—the way the ant had gone in remote times, and in which it had endured as a monumental warning to men?

He was followed by grave, assenting voices to which there is no occasion to listen. "Let the dead bury their dead," is a good text.

With the living we may be concerned, and Wyndham Smith was alive. He had seen in this council meeting an interval during which he would be as entirely alone as though he were already the only man in the world, and it was upon this he had relied for the success of the plan, at once audacious and simple, for Vinetta's rescue.

This was no more than to enter the euthanasia furnace at a time when he knew that he would be unobserved, and hide among the dense greenery of the inner hothouses, from which position he could watch the approach of Vinetta's couch, snatch her from it, and either remain hidden there, or, if there should be interference after her empty couch should have reached the antechamber of death (where it could be observed from outside), to defend her against such as might still be alive, and of a disposition for violence.

He calculated that there could not be more than fifty-five (including eighteen women) who would be alive when he should attempt the rescue, and of these not less than five would have already entered the furnace, and more would have drugged themselves before discovery could be made.

His hope went farther than that. Was it certain that, with so few alive, there would be any watchers who would observe the emptiness of that slow-moving couch? Well, perhaps he must answer yes to that. It would still be more likely than not, even apart from the possibility that there might be a special curiosity to see her pass into the fire. But, even so, when he went over the list of those who would be alive, it was hard to think of them as engaging in a physical struggle, or putting aside the pleasant form of dissolution which was so near, to face with weaponless hands the thrusts of that broad and most deathly blade.

In fact, when he considered what they would do, imagination was baffled. He could not even make a probable guess, but he knew what he would do himself, with Vinetta's life as the stake, and it was likely to be unpleasant for them.

So he entered and hid. He had calculated that he would have to wait until the immolations began, and then for about four hours, but he had attached little importance to that. He knew it to be no more than the beginning of irregularities of living, many of which might involve more serious discomforts or dangers than waiting for five or six hours behind a cover of broad-leaved plants.

He had even had foresight to provide himself with food which could be eaten during the hours of vigil. It was strange to have to think, for the first time in his life, of the need of providing food before the hour of hunger should come! Always, it had appeared before him, the nursery experiences of barbarous times being continued till death in the life he knew. But now the last meal that would be served to mankind by its subservient machines had been distributed and consumed. That had been in the morning. It had been decided that the evening meal would not be required.

* * * * * * *

The first hour passed quickly enough, and with little discomfort. For that time, he was not even careful to conceal himself, knowing that he could not he seen except by those who would pass him on their way to death, and that procession had not yet begun. Actually, when it did, the need for concealment was not much, for those who lay on the passing couches were already stupefied by the drug they had swallowed, and even if they had perceived and recognized him, were in no condition to return to give the alarm. But by that time his own condition had become little better than theirs.

He had noticed as he entered, the heavy, alluring, sickly scent of the flowers blooming on the vines that spread over and hung down from the trellised roof. It was strange to him, for the flowers were grown in no other place, and he had not previously penetrated so far into these portals of death. The flowers were large, with single, wide-open petals, wax-white, with blotches of dark brown on their upper, and a fierce orange colour on their under sides. The scent was unlike anything he had encountered before. Different from, and much more powerful than, that of the outer conservatories.

After a time he ceased to notice it, though its effect did not lessen for that. He became conscious of increasing torpor of body, and difficulty in maintaining connected thought.

He did not know how much this might be due to the heavy, sensuous odour, or how much to the hot, damp air which his body, having been accustomed from birth to dry, equable, temperate warmth, was ill-prepared to endure. He became sharply afraid that, as the hours passed, he might be subdued by these conditions, so that he would be unfit for the rescue which he had planned

He imagined himself lying unconscious while Vinetta would pass on the way of death, and waking too late, to know that he had failed her, and that he would be alone indeed in an empty world. Or perhaps he would never wake. Perhaps he would lie there, unconscious or dead, until, as he knew would be the case two days at the most, the intended fire would spread through the building, consuming that which could no longer be useful to man. His mind wandered from this thought to consider the need for conserving fire in some crude form in the life which was before him now. But perhaps it would be simple enough. Was there not a volcano near the place where he was intending to live? He believed vaguely that they were sources of perpetual fire.

He pulled himself up in abrupt panic to recall what he had been thinking before. Something more important than that. Why did his thoughts wander in this impotent aimless way? He had been thinking of Vinetta, of course. Of how she might lie on her moving litter, fearing, wondering, *trusting* that his rescue would not be delayed, till it would be too late.

Could he fail her thus? Suppose she should see him lie unconscious? Would she not spring up at the sight, and might not the position be saved, even then. If that were so, would it not be better for him to risk being seen by those who would pass earlier, and remain in the open passage between the palms?

But she might herself be too dazed to observe him, too drugged to rise? No, he thought not. She would avoid swallowing the drug. Certainly she would not do so to a deadening quantity. He saw hope here, for the others might pass him in stupefied oblivion, while she might be alert. But, if so, and she should not observe him, or fall to rise, might it not mean that she would be defenceless against the flames?

He imagined her, like Sinto-T9R, aware too late of the horror to which she had been betrayed, and writhing in the flame of her burning robe. Trust in him, obedience to his whispered word, would have brought her to that!

Love of life, which his ego had brought from a remote time, was strengthened by consciousness of the supreme issues involved. He remembered that his honour was pledged; he thought of Vinetta, and love and pity became the most potent forces of all in a prolonged struggle against the languorous poison which remained neither lost nor won.

He thought, as his senses wavered towards unconsciousness narrowly kept at bay, that he might endure better if he could quench the thirst which was increasingly difficult to endure, and he saw a possibility of that, if he should have courage to outrage all the teachings of youth by interfering with a machine.

The automaton whose duty it was to investigate the drying of the soil in the great pots and report to its comrade, who would give them what they required, had recently finished its round. It lay at ease near him at the side of the path, cleaning its proboscis in the thorough leisurely manner which was characteristic of all the machinery of this age, for though they might design each other, as they largely did, the first to be designed came from human brains, which had given their own characteristics to them.

Its companion, having been informed of the quantity of water which would be required, had filled itself to that amount, and now came crawling along the passage, where it halted its laden belly, stretched out a very long, flexible neck that sought among the great pots for those to whom it had been instructed to minister, and commenced to give them the quantities of water that they required. Why, Wyndham thought, should he not divert that injecting nozzle to his own mouth? If a plant should go dry in consequence, surely it would be a triviality, especially as it was doomed to destruction within the week? He put the inhibitions of childish days firmly aside.

He made difficult way along and over the pots, breaking through ruthlessly where he could not otherwise pass, until he came to where that long neck advanced like a lengthening worm to one that was much smaller than those around it. He could not guess that his life hung upon the smallness of that pot.

He caught the flexible, twisting neck in his hands, endeavouring to draw the mouth-like nozzle to his own lips, and was surprised to be opposed by a stubborn strength which his utmost effort could not overcome.

An engineer, soothing it with discriminating fingers, could have compelled it to the desired obedience, but he lacked the knowledge which the position required.

Yet, though he loosed it, he did not resign the effort. He saw that it would only release its water at the places to which it had been directed, and so, bending down, he advanced his own mouth to the nozzle above the surface of the pot.

The next moment he fell back, as the nozzle was pushed forward into his throat with an injection of choking violence.

He rose spitting out water of a foul and poisonous taste, much of which had been forced down his throat by the premature violence with which the automaton had been irritated to act. He had not guessed that it was not pure water, but a liquid plant food, which he was attempting to drink, and of which a large quantity had been forced into his gullet.

Ceasing to spit water, he spat blood from a throat that was bruised and torn. After that, he vomited violently, which may have been a good thing, probably saving his life, but he did not regard it in that way.

Had he been in a mood for such reflections, he might have considered it to be a warning of what the life he had chosen was likely to be. It was an experience as new as it was foul. He had never done such a thing before, never seen it, scarcely knew that it could be. But it had the immediate effect of rousing him from the control of that deadening scent, so that he might have thanked it doubly both for relieving him from the poison he had swallowed, and the most dangerous lethargy against which he had made no more than a losing battle before.

This upheaval of body and mind was scarcely over when he became conscious of sounds which warned him that the first arrivals of the final hundred were entering the furnace, and he withdrew to the shelter the leaves supplied. Near him the automaton stretched its long neck in a helpless manner, vomiting a stream of foul water across the floor. Either the wrench he had first given, or his subsequent action, had caused it to lose the sense of direction which enabled it to find the pots to which it had been directed by its companion.

After an abortive effort, which resulted in nothing better than striking down at the hard floor, it had given up the attempt, and commenced to belch out indiscriminately the contents of its distant belly. Wyndham observed the truth of his childhood's lesson—interfere with a machine, and no one could foretell what it would do. Well, they could go on their own way now, and make way for a more primitive, simpler world!

One by one, at intervals of five or six minutes, the laden couches began to pass; soon after, at similar intervals, the furnace would flare up, as a victim was received through its open doors. The glare which shone into the highly heated anteroom was reflected through the doors of non-inflammable glass, into the hothouse in which Wyndham hid; its roar could be heard by him at such moments more distinctly than it came to those who loitered outside.

He knew that he had still hours to wait, and, as he recovered from the physical shock he had endured, he became apprehensive again of the effect of the deadening scent. He saw that he must face a much longer ordeal than he had yet had. But he found that he was assisted by some freshness of air that came through the opening of doors. Every six minutes the door through which he had come would slide open for a couch to pass, and a breath of dry air would follow, which felt cool and life-giving to him. Every two minutes after, the further door would slide open, bringing an influx of hot air, hard to breathe, but still free from the heavy scent, and, half stupefied though he was, with these helps he endured.

He did not observe that any of those who passed accelerated their own transit, nor that they retarded it, to the delaying of those behind. They appeared to accept the pace at which the cable drew them forward, lying dormantly, so that their degree of consciousness was not easy to judge; but it was certain that they took no notice of him, even when he came venturesomely out, to take fuller advantage of those short-lived currents of cooler air.

So the time passed, until the moment came when Vinetta would be due to appear on the next couch. All his life, Colpeck-4XP had been sheltered from apprehension of disaster, from occasion for fear. But Wyndham felt fear now. He learned anxiety, as he had not yet done, even in the last days.

Would she come? Would they have played some cunning trick? Would she be already too overcome to rise, so that he would be burdened by her insensible form in whatever struggle for her release might be upon him in the next hour? *Would she be already dead?* Suppose they had made certain of their own will by administering—perhaps without arousing her suspicion—some sudden poison? If they had, he resolved that he would sally out and deal such vengeance to those concerned as is possible to wreak on men who are seeking death in the next hour. Now she had come through the open door. He scarcely waited until it closed before his arms were round her and he had lifted her from the couch, which moved on, being so lightened, at a slightly faster pace than previously.

She hung heavily on his arm, so that he saw she was unable to stand on unsteady feet. She looked at him with brave eyes that were yet dazed, fighting with sleep. She said, "I will not doubt. He must have a plan," as though repeating words that she had said to herself before, and not being yet conscious of where she was.

He answered her in exultant confidence, born of what seemed to be an easy success, "So I had. You are safe now," but the puzzled look did not leave her eyes. In fact she was unsure whether she were awake or under the power of a drug-bought dream.

Kisses had more effect. Her eyes changed. She spoke in a more natural voice. "I had to swallow some. They watched all that I did. I could not tell what you meant me to do."

"It is over now. You are safe. We must stay here for a few hours, and after that we shall be free."

So it seemed obvious that they should do. While they talked, two subsequent couches had passed them, the occupants of which had shown no interest in, no awareness of their existence. Even though it should be observed when her couch reached the anteroom that Vinetta had left it, it might appear better to wait the event where they were than to expose themselves, and challenge opposition, by walking out. Every couch that passed them reduced by one, woman or man, the number of their potential foes. Why hasten the event while time so steadily shortened in their favour the still desperate odds?

So they stayed for the next hour, and saw eleven more of the last hundred glide forward to the resolving fire, but by that time the difficulty of retaining consciousness had become so great that it was evident that another five hours of that atmosphere would be beyond mortal endurance. For some time Wyndham had been comparing the advantage of the numerical reduction that they were witnessing with the disadvantage of his own dizzying brain. He did not wish to stagger out so dazed that he would fumble in vain for the hilt of that strange weapon against his thigh. Now Vinetta said, "I am getting so that I cannot stand. If you delay more, you must leave me here. Is there nowhere else we can hide?"

She knew the words to be foolish as she uttered them. To go forward was to enter the anteroom, where, as the emptiness of her couch appeared to have been unobserved, it was possible that they also might not be under instant observation, but they knew that the heat, even at the near end, would be beyond endurance. On the side nearer the furnace it would be so great that their garments would burst into flame. How much they would feel it they could not tell, nor what the pain of burning would be, which was outside their experience; but they knew that it would be sufficient to damage their bodies beyond repair.

To go back would be to enter the cooler greeneries which were under observation both by those outside, and any who might be entering and still in possession of their normal senses.

The place where they were was the only part of the way of death which was not open to outside observation, and that was solely because the density of the tropic plants blinded the heat-proof glass. It was also the only section that was not artificially lighted. Light entered from either end, and above a full moon shone through the glass roof.

Being unable longer to endure the atmosphere where they were, they took the only possible course when they went back, and they used such prudence as the position allowed when they halted in the corridor through which the couches commenced their journey. Here they were in full view of those who were taking their final draught, and would have been from the outside also, had any been there to see, but they did not go out among them immediately. They paused in the purer, cooler air, drawing in breaths that restored them to something which approached their natural vitality before they were subject to more than the curious glances of those who remained alive.

CHAPTER TWENTY-ONE

For the reason that Munzo-D7D and Pilwin-C6P had kept their suspicions secret—Avanah-F3B had already entered the furnace—the appearance of Vinetta was a matter of blank surprise to all but these two, but it didn't require that they should be—as they were—the best brains of that dying world for them to be able to guess what its meaning was. They saw the whole declared purpose for which they, with five millions of their fellows, had undertaken that procession of death reduced to mockery by the treacherous defiance of a single woman. It was not surprising that murmurs rose.

It may be hard to guess to what these would have led had they been left to their own courses, but Pilwin asked, "Shall I warn him of what he does?" And Munzo, having replied, "It would be an act of kindness, which he would thank," moved among his companions with reassuring words, so that they continued the orderly process of that on which they were engaged, only turning curious eyes to where Pilwin-C6P could be seen in conversation with Colpeck-4XP, which, from earnestness, developed an evident anger, and then a sight so unprecedented and incredible that men might ask themselves whether they had not already passed from the living world to such vivid dreams as dissolution by fire may give.

"I have come," Pilwin-C6P commenced, looking at Vinetta as he spoke, though the words might be meant for both, "to warn you in friendly words, while there is still time to avoid the horror to which you go."

"As to that," Wyndham replied, with deliberation, feeling that every passing second was gain to him, both to fill his lungs, and for the number of those who might obstruct his purpose to reduce themselves, "we thank you, being content to believe that your purpose is friendly to us, but we have made our choice, and ask no more than to be left alone to bring it to the best end that we can."

"I am not greatly concerned for you," Pilwin replied, with no friendliness in his voice. "You have made deliberate choice, knowing what you do, which had the council's assent. But you have persuaded Vinetta to attempt that which will bring her to a most dreadful death, which there is still time to avoid, if she will go the way which wisdom points, and which her honour requires."

Hearing this, Wyndham was moved both to anger and fear on behalf of the woman he had come so nearly to save, for he resented the implication that he had persuaded her to dishonour herself, and knew Pilwin-C6P well enough to judge that he would not have said what he did without confident belief in the warning his words conveyed. He replied, "As to her honour, I should say it would be hard to find, if she should join you in the most craven act that the earth has known. And will you tell me what your laws will be worth by tomorrow's dawn? It will be for the living to make their own. But I am more concerned to know what you may mean when you talk of Vinetta being near to a dreadful death, which we must know how to avoid. Having said so much, I will ask you to tell me that."

"That is more than I have permission to do."

"Permission from whom? The council could have resolved nothing without our knowledge and there can be no other permission you need to have."

Pilwin did not argue this. He replied, "It would make no difference if I did, for it is a death impossible to avoid, and too late to change."

"I prefer to judge that for myself. Having said so much, you must say more."

"What I say is that Vinetta must go the way of her kind, or a time will soon come when she will curse you for persuading her to a worse end."

"You have done, I suppose, some devilish thing, and I will know what it is though I pull the tongue from your mouth."

Pilwin-C6P did not actually think of being personally assaulted. The man who confronted him was Colpeck-4XP, whom he had known from childhood, and the idea of a violent scuffle developing between them seemed—as it should have been a week earlier—too grotesque for a waking dream. But he did not like the look in his antagonist's eyes, and instinct, stronger than reason or experience, caused him to take a backward step even as this threat was spoken, and that step was the signal for Wyndham's leap.

It was not a fight. It was rather an all-in wrestling match of great energy and supreme incompetence. The two bodies, superbly gymnasium-trained, were yet utterly without practice in any contests or trials of skill with those of their own kind, which had been prohibited by law, as involving the element of competition and the necessary consequence that some would be defeated, as others won.

The course of events would have been by a different route to the same end, had Wyndham remembered his Roman sword, but he was not seeking to kill. He aimed to force confession from reluctant lips, and he obeyed blind, primitive instinct when he leaped at his opponent's throat, as his barbarous ego would be likely to do.

Instinct, equally atavistic, prompted Pilwin's resistance, but strength of purpose, and impulses of anger and fear, were on Wyndham's side, as was the fact that his body, for several days, had been releasing itself from the tyranny of the deadening drug. For the first moments, the advantage was his.

He brought Pilwin to the ground. He caught him by the hair, striking his face. "Will you speak now?"

Pilwin felt no pain from the blows he took. He might not yet be experiencing the full effects of the final draught which he and his companions had just taken, but his daily dosage gave him sufficient immunity against superficial pains. His answer was to clutch at a foot which was driven sharply into his ribs. He pulled Wyndham down. The two men rolled on the floor.

Pilwin tried to rise, and Wyndham to beat him back. Their single garments were torn away. Pilwin was left nearly naked: purple shreds of cloth trailed grotesquely from the sword-belt which Wyndham wore. The sword itself had slipped from a sheath where it had only loosely lain, and fallen upon the ground.

Vinetta watched the struggle without offering assistance. She did not stand back either from timidity or reluctance to interfere, or because she thought it a man's part to fight in a woman's cause. The etiquette of the event did not enter her mind. She was, in fact, more completely freed, even than Wyndham, from any sense of loyalty to her kind, or their customs, or dying laws. Her loyalty was to him alone, her thought was single that she fought for her life against desperate odds, and if it should be lost in the end, it would be through no foolish scruple of hers. But she thought shrewdly that if she should make any motion to interfere, others might do the same, and the odds would be no better for that. Only, when she saw Wyndham's leg move on the floor perilously near to the bare blade, she stepped forward and picked it up.

She hated Pilwin-C6P, as she had reason to do; there was only Munzo-D7D whom she hated more. She would have been glad to see Wyndham break him in some fatal way, but she understood that they must aim at a smaller thing. They must make him tell, if they could, that which it was vital for her to know.

So, having confidence in her companion, she looked on for the first minute, quietly content; but the next waked her to an unwelcome sight. She was cool-witted enough to see that Wyndham was not having the best of the bout. The fact was that his experiences of the last seven hours, the swallowing of that foul water, the vomiting, the enervating endurance of the scent-laden atmosphere of the hothouse, had rendered him less fit than his opponent for a prolonged struggle, of which he became aware as the first impulse of anger spent itself on one whom it had battered, but who did not yield.

Less drugged than Pilwin in another way, he felt the pain of the hurts he took, though it may be doubted whether there were disadvantage in that. He became aware that, in spite of his utmost effort, Pilwin would be likely to break away, and with this realization his purpose changed. He remembered that Munzo-D7D was looking on. Doubtless he also knew of the trap which had been set for Vinetta's life. Let him see an example of what befell one who refused to speak!

He looked up at Vinetta; their eyes met, and she understood that he asked her aid. There came to his mind what the curator of the museum had told him of how the Roman soldier was taught to thrust upward under his convex shield. With a supreme effort, he dragged Pilwin down. He got his knee sideways across his throat. "In his belly," he gasped. "Push it up." Would she never do it? Every second it seemed impossible that he could retain his grip of the writhing man. He was breaking loose. He was down again. Wyndham knew it to be the last supreme effort that he could make. Frantic hands grappled and strained and tore.

Vinetta was not aware of any slowness in what she did. She was instant to catch the meaning of the glance, and the gasped words. Coolly watching her chance, as her feet moved slightly at the side of the writhing man, she pushed in the short broad blade with so firm a thrust that there was little but the hilt that remained in view.

Pilwin felt no pain. He did not know the nature of his own hurt. But he gave a terrible choking cry. His body moved convulsively, and Wyndham felt its muscles relax. Breathing hard, he relaxed himself from an effort such as is only possible when the issue is life or death. He heard Vinetta's voice asking, in a controlled excitement, "Is it enough? Shall I pull it out?"

CHAPTER TWENTY-TWO

Munzo-D7D watched the scuffling men, and was not greatly concerned. It was a ridiculous, ignominious exhibition, but it had been Pilwin's own idea that he should interfere with advice which it was not necessary to give, and which had evidently been ill received. If he got hurt—or perhaps damaged would be the better word, the question of acute pain being remote—it could hardly be a matter of great concern to others who were now assembled with him to pass the portals of death. Still less would Munzo's mind be disturbed if the barbarian should limp away with a laming wound. And as to Vinetta, her fate was already settled.

It had always been a weakness with Pilwin-C6P that he would find reasons for doing things rather than for letting them remain. It had been the proverbial fault of all who had borne the Pilwin name for six generations past. Let him kick or be kicked, it did not occur to Munzo-D7D to lift a finger, or suggest that other fingers should be lifted for him. Rather, if he showed any concern, it was to hold back those who looked on at so strange a sight, that they should not further impair the dignity of this culminating moment of human fate.

Such, at least, was his attitude while the two men struggled upon the ground. The nature of Vinetta's inter-position was not clearly seen, nor its significance understood, until Wyndham rose breathlessly from a foe who was making no more than convulsive writhings amid a pool of blood which spread from the hilt of a weapon driven so deeply that its blunt-shaped point was out two inches beside his spine.

"Yes," Wyndham said, "pull it out. We do not know how quickly we may want it again." For the moment, he could scarcely see steadily, he could scarcely stand, so great had the effort been which had held his foe for that fatal thrust.

Vinetta pulled out the sword, which she found, surprisingly hard. Doing it, she was deluged with blood, which shot upward to spray the leaves of the path-side plants.

Wyndham took it from her hands. His sight was steadying now. "You did well," he said. "In another moment I must have let go."

"But how you held him!" she replied. "It was long enough." Admiration was in her eyes.

She looked down on a dying foe, and her glance changed to a pitiless contempt of one who showed symmetry of muscular form with which few Greek statues could have compared. So, for that matter, did the man at her side. She would have said that she had good reason to hate. Those who had killed her mother, who would have destroyed her also had they been as sure of her identity as she now was in her own mind—what loyalty did she owe them? Had she ever owed? They went the way they chose, and she might have said that they chose well. And one lay thus who had practiced against her life in a way which might still bring her to bitter death. Could she have less than satisfaction in that?

Their eyes turned from the dying man to the little crowd who watched them through the open archway. Even those who had been occupied with their last meal had risen to regard this final episode in the history of their race, after they had supposed that the last word had been said, and the curtain begun to fall.

Wyndham saw Munzo-D7D in the centre of those who were most advanced. He said, "There he is." Ignoring the others, he advanced upon him, the bloody sword in his hand. Munzo's indifference had already changed to apprehensive doubt, as he had seen the state to which Pilwin's twitching body had been reduced. There were many barbarians of Wyndham's own twentieth century to whom it would have been an unpleasant sight, though they were used to scenes of violence and death, to crushing each other on bloody roads, and to hanging the disembowelled carcasses of other animals very similar to themselves along the side of their public streets. But to these people it was an exhibition revolting almost beyond endurance to see, and intolerable to imagine as an ignominy which their own bodies might be about to suffer.

Munzo-D7D had no inclination to await a conversation which might end with him sprawling in the same way, with his own entrails protruding in that ghastly manner. The thought of resistance, single or in combination with his fellows, did not enter his mind. He thought only of how he might reach the furnace which would give him release in the decent, dignified manner his civilization required without encountering that advancing sword.

The problem might have appeared difficult to some, Wyndham being between him and the only corridor of approach, but he had the best brains of his time, and it was a question of mathematics which he had no difficulty in solving in a simple manner. He turned, and, as he did so, said to those around him, "Do not fear. It is I whom he seeks." Then he retreated quickly through the outer door.

Wyndham saw his movement, and followed, as he had been expected to do. The group of those between them, reassured by Munzo's words, did not imitate his flight. They served slightly to hinder Wyndham's pursuit, though not much, drawing quickly to right and left, as Munzo had foreseen that they would. He wanted sufficient start, but yet to ensure that Wyndham would follow at no great distance.

So he did. Vinetta, close behind, would have stopped him if she could, but she called words which he did not hear. Her mind held singly to the one point. Munzo-D7D must be kept alive, that he might be made to talk. Let him be kept outside the furnace while the rest should go to their deaths, and they would have him safely enough. Besides that, she feared to be distant from Wyndham's side. The threat was not to both. It was single to her. Her only hope was in him. So, as she could not stay him, she went the same way.

Munzo, seeing he was pursued, began to run at his best pace. He knew that Wyndham could run faster than he, but the distance in his mind was not great, and he thought that he had sufficient start.

So it proved. He ran with the speed of a desperate man. He was resentfully aware that he occupied his last hour in an absurd way, but he sacrificed his dignity in a small matter, that he might save it in a larger.

Wyndham's recent occupation had not been the best possible preparation for such a pursuit, but he was younger, and he also was in the mood from which exceptional effort is born. For the length of the building he followed Munzo, who could be clearly seen on the white, moonlit pavement, content to know that he was gaining at every stride. But when Munzo turned under the furnace wall, and returned along its further side, Wyndham increased his effort, seeing how he had been fooled, and guessing the purpose in Munzo's mind.

When Munzo got back to the door he had left, Wyndham was not more than three or four yards behind. Munzo burst through the group of those who stood uncertainly there. He called, "Follow me to the way of a clean death."

These words, and the sight of Wyndham's approaching sword, had the effect on which Munzo relied. The little crowd closed behind, following his flight towards the inner chambers, and impeding Wyndham's pursuit.

Wyndham's voice was furious on their rear. "Fools, let me pass! It is not you that I seek." Words failing to clear his way, he tried what the sword would do. One man fell with a cleft head, having no need to run farther to find his death. But the others scrambled on the faster for that, as he might have guessed that they would. They passed through the hothouse corridor, a jostling, screaming crew, frantic in flight, with Wyndham's sword jabbing, upon their rear.

Spreading out in the hot antechamber of death, they left the way to Munzo open at last, but it was too late to be of any avail. Fortunate in his sensitiveness to pain, Wyndham became aware that every step towards the furnace encountered a fiercer heat. He stopped, and as he did so became aware of Vinetta's hand on his arm pulling him back.

"You cannot help me now," she said; "but that is no reason that you should die."

They saw Munzo, his robe flaring around his shoulders, still running on to the furnace as swiftly as his tired legs could be made to move, while his lungs were scorched by the heated air. He had had the wit to perceive that, if he did not urge his steps with his dying will, he might not reach the furnace at all, and he was still anxious to end in a seemly manner.

Some of those who followed were less wise or less resolved in what they did. They fell round the furnace threshold, roasting and smoking there.

Wyndham, looking at the end of the race to which he had so strangely come, was moved to a gust of laughter that the roaring furnace could not consume.

Homeric laughter, peal on peal, shook the heated air of the antechamber, and might be thought no unfitting requiem of the race of men, or introduction of their craven souls to the Ultimate Reality they had gone to face.

But Vinetta did not laugh. She said, with an excusable note of bitterness in her voice, "Well, I hope you know how you can save me now!"

Munzo-D7D might have retorted to that mocking hilarity with the proverb that he laughs longest who laughs last, but that he was no longer in condition to make retort on any earthly occasion; and, besides, it was a proverb he had not known.

CHAPTER TWENTY-THREE

Wyndham looked at the hand that was still on his arm, and that had drawn him back none too soon, for he was aware that his whole body was scorched and dry. He placed his own hand upon hers. "We have come through more," he said, "than we thought we should. We shall find a way."

She was not without courage, as has been seen. She took what comfort she could from confident words.

They went back, with linked arms and hands, at a slower pace than they had come.

In the hothouse corridor, where they spent too much time before, they found that, when they thought that they were left alone in an empty world, they had assumed more than was true.

A black-browed woman, Swartz-02A, had been thrown aside in the rush, and was now rising, on unsteady feet, dazed from a head-wound, the cause of which was shown by the broken side of one of the pots. Blood ran from her short-cropped hair, and dropped from a damaged ear.

Wyndham looked at her doubtfully. Were there to be three, rather than two? It was a thought that he did not like, though he could see advantages, more than one.

Vinetta looked, and her doubt was of another kind. She saw a woman against whom she had nursed for years a hate that she must not show, for the records said that Swartz-02A had been active, not merely to vote—as all had—but to argue for her mother's death. "Why," she thought, "should Pilwin's belly be slit, and hers whole?" Well, there had been a present reason for that.

"She seems too stupid to move," Vinetta said. "She had better follow her friends." With firm hands, though without roughness, she pulled off the woman's outer cloak. Then Vinetta put on the woman's cloak and slipped off her own garment from beneath it.

They drew her into the hot antechamber, where there was now a smell of roasting flesh such as would have been pleasant to twentieth-century nostrils, but was nauseous to theirs, taking her as near to the furnace as their own skins would endure. They withdrew in haste from the scorching heat, and looked back to see that she had not moved.

"We can't leave her there. She will only scorch," Vinetta said doubtfully. Feeling the heat as they did, it was hard to think of others as being immune from the dreadful pain. Certainly, it was not pleasant to think of the woman walking blindly away from the central heat, and waking to further consciousness in a half-roasted condition on the next day.

There was a rough mercy in what he did when Wyndham, completing a series of actions of the possibility of which Colpeck-4XP would not have thought in his wildest dream, ran forward into the heat, and with a hard kick sent the woman, stumbling and sprawling forward to fall among those who were already roasted flesh at the furnace-mouth.

As he rejoined Vinetta she turned away. "Come," she said, "we have lost too much time now."

"I don't want to stay here," he said. "I hope we may never see such a place again. But why did you want the woman's robe? We can get all you care to take."

He had loaded the aeroplane with such things as seemed likely to be useful to him or them, omitting only such as were specifically feminine, which he had not ventured to take. His plan had been that they should add such articles as she chose in the hours before morning came.

But she was now in an urgent haste to be gone, thinking that the threat to her own life of which Pilwin-C6P had spoken in such ominous words must be something close around, which they might avoid by a rapid flight. She did not think it could be any trick which would wreck the plane, for it had been clear that it was against her only that it was aimed, and anything of that kind would apparently have been equally fatal to Wyndham, even had she gone the way of obedient death.

Wyndham did not object to the haste she showed. The value she put on her own life did not price it more highly than he, and they both knew that whatever had seemed certain to the two by whom it had been contrived would not be easily foiled.

"In any case," Wyndham said, "the garments are of little account.

He meant that the only difference between those worn by men and women had been that the woman's purple was of a darker shade, and he had stored a supply for his own use. The need of that differing shade would not be much from this hour!

With sufficient moonlight on smooth, white paths, they went to the place—it was no more than half a mile distant—where the aeroplane lay. They went by a quiet desolate road, but with hearts beating with vague fear, and apprehensive eyes searching the gloom. The warning of Pilwin-C6P was potent already to spoil the peace of the new life which, without that, would have had perils and problems enough.

But nothing happened at all. The night was quiet and vacant around them. They looked back to the community buildings, which were lit up to the extent which was usual during the darker hours So far they had not deviated from their routine through the absence of the human residents by whom they had been designed and controlled. But that collapse would be sure to come.

The aeroplane was easy to find, having lit itself, as its duty was, when the night had come. It required no pilot, and it was not usual for it to carry living passengers, but its design had been partially governed by the habits of earlier centuries. It was more bird-like in form than the first aeroplanes, having a head which had once been a passenger-cabin *de luxe*, as it would, retain a level floor even when the body swerved or dived in the wild skies of those early days.

Its wings also moved in a bird-like manner, spreading more widely for increase of speed, and flapping regularly, for it was with these that it flew, rather than with its tail, which was used for steering only.

Seen from below its wings appeared to move with no more than a sluggish ease, like those of a heron in lazy flight, but they could propel it at a great speed through the windless skies. Its engines were soundless, which increased the illusion of living wings. Under normal conditions of flight it was of an absolute safety. There was no record of accident to any aeroplane which had been sent aloft since the skies were tamed. How it would behave if tempests should sweep again through the upper air was less easy to judge, which was another reason why Wyndham was content to agree to an instant start.

But literally instantly, they found that it could not be. The controls in the head-cabin, which were intended to be worked while it was still on the ground, were clearly marked, and their directions were explicit. Its destination must be set as the starting lever was moved. On that lever being turned over, it would occupy itself in taking in fuel and oil, and in testing its vital parts for a period which would not be less than twenty minutes, and might be much longer if it should discover any defect such as might require the substitution of a duplicate part. For it was constructed to test and repair itself or, at the worst, to indicate that it was unfit for flight and must submit to the care of the hospital sheds, where machines of greater competence would operate upon it.

"I agreed," Wyndham said, "with Pilwin, that I would go to Mount Ida, which he strongly recommended as a place where, though I might not live, I should take longer to die."

"It sounds a good choice," she replied doubtfully, "and is a long distance from there."

"So it may be. But I was not sure then that Pilwin was thinking only of me, and I am more doubtful now."

He looked at the direction controls, which showed that there were no less than twenty stations to which the aeroplane could be set to alight. The third was Mount Ida. His eye passed on rapidly. He knew what he looked for, his decision being already made. He raised his hand to the ninth, *Taormina*, and turned it over before she could protest.

She looked at it and him with contracted brows. "Well," she said, "it is done now" She knew that the destination could not be altered when it had once been set. "Of course, it is a place they will never guess. But have you thought of the mists? Could we live through them?"

She thought his action showed that he would sacrifice everything for her, as he might have done, but in this choice he had thought of more than had yet come to her mind.

CHAPTER TWENTY-FOUR

The winds and weather were now controlled to an extent that ensured equable temperature and peaceful skies in all places which had been the regular abodes of men, but the effect of the equinoxes remained, and some differences between winter and summer in the two hemispheres there had still been. The effects of reduced hours of sunlight in the northern winter had been corrected by wind currents, which left the Mediterranean a stagnant area hidden in mist for six months of the year. There was no trouble for that.

The sea was vacant, since men had ceased the folly of moving vainly about. No one dwelt on its shores. Only, in some parts of Sicily, the cultivation of grapes had been allowed to continue during the summer of sunny days, and of regulated rain during the nights. They had been tended entirely by automata, which could dig and plant, and in due season gather the crop, and load it for transport to the central food-depot in Hungary. Men might not have visited it at all during recent years.

Wyndham had disregarded the threat of the Mediterranean mists. He had enquired what the climate of Sicily had been in the ancient days. Such he supposed it would be again when the winds were free. He had learned from the librarian that it had been temperate in winter, and that it was sufficiently mountainous to allow them, as he rather crudely dreamed, to mitigate the effect of seasonal changes by climbing up to the heights, or moving down to the shore-levels. It had an active volcano, to which he also attached a theoretical importance which might be modified by experience.

Finally, though it was an island, it was no longer detached from the mainland. The old Messina ferry had been replaced by an enormous concrete causeway. The power of Etna in stimulated eruption had been harnessed to this gigantic task about two centuries earlier. The librarian could not say that it had been visited by any of the present generation, but there could be no doubt that it still stood in that windless sea.

Wyndham's imagination, inflamed by Avanah's historical tales, had gone forward to vague dreams of an earth released again to renewed riot of life, swarming with greater beasts, perhaps including some of semi-human character, against which his descendents, multiplying themselves in that spacious island, would erect an impregnable barrier where the causeway joined the land. They would be secure in their island home, and yet free, as the centuries would pass, to sally out to win a wider domain.

Something of this he said, while they waited in the aeroplane cabin, and heard within its entrails the noises of the preparations it made for the coming flight. They had secured the door by which they had entered. They could do no more to safeguard her life from a danger the nature of which they could not guess, nor from what direction it would arrive; and the spacious dream did something to turn her mind from its present fear.

It was an hour before dawn when the plane gently and steadily lifted its bird-like head, and began to move forward along the ground. Quickly the pace increased. The wings lifted. Before its course the ground dipped sharply, and as it did so the plane rose, with a rapid flapping of wide-spread wings.

The dim bulk of the buildings, in which they had passed the whole of their pain-free, negative lives till that hour, showed beside and then beneath them in the level light of the setting moon. That sight, at least, had gone forever from mortal eyes, as had the dull glow of the euthanasia furnace which held the ashes, or was still baking the flesh, of the ninety-eight with whom they had ruled the world to so vain an end. The steady wing-beats bore them onward and up, under the starry vault of a cloudless sky. On the far low horizon to which they flew there was the first faint hint of the coming dawn.

The main cabin—the upper body, as it were, of the great bird—was plainly meant only for transit of goods, for the safe reception of which it was fitted with large cupboards and shelves, bars and ropes and hanging straps, and fixed grooves along which sliding partitions might be run, as the nature and quantity of its cargo required. Beneath, in a lower compartment, were the engines and all the complicated mechanism of flight. Only the small head—cabin had been adapted for the human occupants for whom it had been originally designed.

The tools and garments, the stores of food, and other articles which Wyndham had collected for his lonely and desperate quest were in the main cabin. The head-cabin, steady in its level flight, as though borne on a sentient neck, and giving wide views above, around, ahead, through transparent panels and roof, was uncumbered, but still allowing little more than comfortable space for them to stand, or stretch themselves on the pneumatic, silk-soft cushions with which it was furnished.

For the moment, a least, they were secure in the safe and lonely heights of the placid air. And they were not merely alive in bodies drugged to a condition of dull existence, scarcely sentient either of pleasure or pain. They were exultantly, passionately alive, and aware of each other, in this great moment, so high, so lonely, so hardly won.

Wyndham cast from him the sword-belt he had ceased to need. He was incredibly careless, for the first time in his ordered life, that he was not free from dirt or the stains of his own and another's blood.

He caught Vinetta in eager arms, and kissed her as they stood beneath the dim light of the stars. A week before, Colpeck-4XP would not have thought such ecstasy as theirs was possible to human kind.

Soon the pale gold of sunrise, which was a familiar monotony of that time of year in the windless skies, broadened and rose wide and high, chasing the stars. But its core was no longer pale. It was an intense crimson, fading upward into a colder gold where the day-star shone. It was such a dawn as she had not seen.

"It is the dawn," she said, in the exultation of the moment through which she came, "of a new world. It may have been so when the world began."

Wyndham lifted his eyes. In the northern sky he saw the long trail of a windy cloud, that drifted over the last of the falling stars. "So it may be," he said. "We will call it a good omen for us. But it may be well that we did not delay till a later hour."

"So it was," she agreed, with another meaning than his. "There is no doubt about that."

He rose to regard further the strange magnificence of the windy dawn, and to guess the meaning of those wisps of clouds in the wide fields of the northern air. He looked down on a barer landscape than had been in the old, disorderly, fecund days, when trees and weeds of little value were left to breed almost at their own wills, and dogs were allowed to live which were of no value or use at all. Bare of life it might be, random or tamed, but its contours were little changed. Its hills rose. Its rivers twisted, thin, silver ribbon beneath the dawn.

The sight to him was almost strange, and recalled something that Munzo-D7D had said to himself at least to Colpeck-4XP—a few months before, which had been accepted at the time as an argument difficult to refute.

He had said that, if the Universe had been the work of a constructive, orderly mind, it would have been more neatly arranged: the stars would have been the same distances apart, and the rivers would have run straight to the sea, with tributaries at right-angles, and at regular intervals. "But everywhere," he had said, "there is disorder and senseless waste, such as would disgrace the brain of a child."

Wyndham recalled this, but a difference of circumstance, or perhaps of ego, caused him to be less friendly to the plausible argument. Certainly it was true that the rivers wandered about, and he had seen before that the stars were strewn as though Blind Chance were their only god. But was it not possible that this was just because they were the work of an Infinite Mind? That it is only the finite brain, capable of no more than a succession of single thoughts, which must have method—and pattern—in its designs, lest they fall—to confusion it cannot rule?

Munzo's idea—as he did not know—was not new. An old, forgotten poet had put it aside by no better device than bold assertion of what was not. "Order," he had written, "is Heaven's first law," to which the obvious comment must be that, if it be so, it is a law which it does not keep.

Wyndham said something of this as he looked down on those twisting rivers, calling Vinetta to share his thought, as it might often become his habit to do, if she should survive the snare by which Munzo-D7D had contrived her death.

And, as might also be a frequent experience, she looked with different eyes, and replied with more practical words. She had been taught, with some detailed exactness, the physical features of the earth, which her occupation had required her to know, and of which his own knowledge was vague and slight. She asked abruptly, "Do you know where we are?"

"Not exactly. Does it matter?"

"But you can see which way we are going! You can see that by the sun."

Yes. He could see that, now he looked with observant eyes. They were flying almost due east. Certainly not a straight way to Taormina, though for Mount Ida it would have been well enough.

That was a fact. But what could they do? If the plane were taking them to another place than that to which it had been set, it was a matter with which they should not venture to interfere. They were faced by the warning not to change the controls after they had been set for flight. The mechanism was not—they could but suppose—intended to be manipulated by a pilot *en route*. No one would normally be with it upon its flights. If Pilwin-C6P had had it manipulated in some manner which would land them where his trap was set, they dare not attempt an interference which, if it were not futile, might lead to disaster they could not guess. The aeroplane, winging its steady way towards the great mountains ahead, became to them as a giant eagle bearing them to its own place like a taken prey.

But what could they do? Nothing, while they remained in those cloudless heights. The aeroplane required no aid from, and might yield no obedience to, them.

Being so impotent to control the event beyond what they had already done, they became aware of the physical ennui that followed a day and night of tension and strife, and many exhausting moods. If they slept now, would they not be more equal to whatever there might be to face when the moment of landing should come? Soon, the plane flew on towards the mountain range that made a late dawn for the climbing sun, and the two who remained alive in a lonely world were unconscious of what it did.

CHAPTER TWENTY-FIVE

"If we be flying east when we wake", they had said, "we shall know Taormina to be a place we shall never see." But when they waked they could tell nothing of that. The sun was hidden above, and the earth beneath. The great bird in whose head they flew was beating wings which were obscured by the driving sleet. The wind was a rushing tempest without, with which the wide-stretched wings strove, beating more rapidly than they had done before. The head-cabin, although the plane was designed to keep it steady, swayed and shook its occupants from their feet, if they rose from the pneumatic cushions without the support of a friendly bar.

To the two who looked, it was a strange and terrible sight, for it was the first time that they had known the forces of wind and rain in insurrection from human control. They had heard of such outbreaks before in most ancient tales, and seen them in pictures that still remained They had no capacity to judge whether the fury they witnessed now were stirred to a dangerous degree, nor knowledge of how far the plane, which had been accustomed to move through a placid air, was adapted to endurance of such conditions.

When the tempest parted for a moment, it showed a pale sun high in the sky, and clouds that raced across it at a fantastic speed. It was not a sufficient glimpse to enable them to judge the direction in which they flew, but it showed them that they were going the way of the wind, which was contrary to what they had supposed.

"I understood," Wyndham said, "from something Pilwin let out, that there would most probably be a great wind from the north. If that be so, we are going in the right direction now."

"It may be only because the plane has been blown off its course, the wind being too strong to face. But are you sure you are right? By the way the sleet falls behind, I should have said we were flying dead into the wind."

"I should say that is because we are leaving the wind behind. We are flying faster than it."

So it was. Whether it had no strength to outface the gale, or because they were both of the same mind, the plane flew the wind's way, and had put on its utmost speed, as though in haste to reach the safety of solid ground before more turmoil should vex the air.

There was no change for the next hour, except that once they had a glimpse, at no great distance beneath, of a most turbulent sea. They could not guess whether they had come so low by the plane's choice, or whether it were being forced down by the elemental violence through which it flew. They took what comfort they could from the thought that, had they continued eastward, land would have been a more likely sight.

After that the plane, no less sensitive to nearness of water or land than if its controls had been subject to the caprices of human hands, soared upward to such a height that they were surrounded by blinding snow. There was no change of temperature in the cabin, but they saw wings and body steam as the ice which had been swiftly forming upon them was melted away.

"I had heard that they used to be fitted with this device," Wyndham said, "though I supposed that it would have been given up, not being required in our day. The upper surfaces heat themselves if the ice form. I suppose we steam overhead in the same way."

"I know little about these planes. If we are heading for Taormina, how soon shall we be due?"

"In about two hours, by a schedule that I saw at the landing ground. Mount Ida, would, of course, be a longer flight. But in this storm? We might either have been blown out of our course, or helped by a following wind so that we should be sooner there."

So they might. They could only wait the event, not knowing the destination which they struggled to reach, nor how far the plane might be equal to the conditions through which it flew. Indeed, as the gale increased to hurricane violence, striving and buffeting the great bird in whose head they still lay till it seemed a miracle that it did not tear off those wide-beating wings, they could not even guess whether they were in exceptional storm, or whether such experiences had been the routine of those who flew in the heavens of ancient days.

They could only comfort themselves with the vague knowledge that the plane was so constructed that it would become aware of, and turn away from, any threatening contact of land or water, except only at the landing-places it knew, to any of which, when it should near them, it would be magnetically drawn in such a way that under peaceful skies, its landing would have been safe and sure.

And the time of waiting was not long, for, a full hour before, by Wyndham's reckoning, they should have been over the Sicilian coast, they became aware that the plane was no longer content to go, more or less, by the way that the tempest drove.

It beat up into the wind, heeling over as it did so until it seemed that one lifted wing pointed to heaven and one earthward into the black abyss of the storm. But even then its head remained little inclined, and in the end it came round with broad wings lying upon the wind.

But if it had intended to plane downward against the strength of the gale, it was a miscalculation of its mechanism which must be changed for a more strenuous descent. It must fight with hard-beating wings for every yard of its downward course, that the hurricane should not sweep it away, until, beneath the barrier of a mountain height that was yet not visible in the storm, it came to a lesser rage of what was still no less than a shrieking gale. Steadily it came to rest on a level place.

The day was still far from spent, but they could see nothing of where they were through that blackness of beating storm. It would have been folly to venture out, even had they been free from the vague terror of Pilwin's threat.

As it was, they barred the only entrance to the interior of the plane, which was at the rear of the main cabin, and waited with what patience they could for the coming of clearer skies.

CHAPTER TWENTY-SIX

Wyndham waked to look up to a blue sky, and a risen sun.

He thought, "Though we die, as it is most likely we shall—and sure at last—in a painful way, we can have no envy for those who have gone to death by a duller road.

Yet he had hope, even that it might not be till a distant day, as he saw that the storm had fallen to nothing more than a strong wind from the north, which swept through an empty sky; and this rose the more when he saw Mount Etna's long snow-topped crest—which he knew from pictures the librarian had brought out, at which he had glanced while he had affected a greater interest in Mount Ida, and other places—looking as though it were no great distance away.

He saw that the plane had been true to the direction that it received, and if Pilwin had baited some cunning trap on the assumption that it would be Mount Ida to which they would take their flight, it might be hoped that it would end in nothing worse than the snapping of empty jaws.

He guessed correctly that, through whatever cause, these automata of the skies did not fly from one station to another by direct routes, but along the lines of invisible rectangles of the air. Their course must have been north-easterly until they had approached the great barrier of the Alps, and then turned southeastward along the course of the Rhone valley, at the time when the mercy of circumstance had brought the full force of the storm upon them from the northwestern quarter.

With the wind's buffeting help they had not merely arrived, but done the distance in one or two hours less than the scheduled time. Their greatest peril, the extremity of which he was unable to judge, had been when it had become necessary to resist the gale and reach the landing-ground in defiance of its furious strength. But the event had proved that these automata had been designed with sufficient subtlety and resource to overcome the caprices of weather which had for so long been banished from peaceful skies.

The thought led him to ponder whether there might not be further use for so efficient a servant. He supposed that this place where it had settled would be provided with reservoirs of fuel and oil from which it would replenish itself, if he should give it the signal to set out on another flight. But he put the idea aside, except for a final extremity. If they should find climatic or other conditions impossible here, or if it should become necessary to flee the nameless terror which still threatened Vinetta's life, it might become wise to fly to a distant place.

But he saw that, two only as they now were in an empty world, they must not seek to find adventures of land or air, but in every way to avoid danger, to play for safety at every point. There would be enough of unavoidable hazard, of difficult chance, that would come to them. It was their part to conserve their own lives until their children should reach sufficient age to be independent of them—and life, so lived, might become very dear, very delightful, in quiet, laborious days—only supposing that Pilwin's words should prove to have been no more than a baseless threat, or to have told of an arrow that missed its mark.

But though the plane might have taken its last flight, and be destined never again to spread its now indrawn wings in the lawless skies, he saw that it might be put to another use.

It would give them shelter, though it would not maintain the equable heat in the living-cabin which had rendered them indifferent to the icy heights through which they had flown. That had been derived from the heat generated in its flight. But it would still be a protection from cold wind or the blaze of a too ardent sun. So he thought, striving to make imagination supply that which experience was unable to yield.

There was security, too, of a kind, in its metal walls, strong though light, and its bolted door. If he only knew the danger from which he must guard her who had become so finally irreplaceable, so inexpressibly dear!

The thought drew his eyes to Vinetta, awakened now and coming into the main cabin.

"It seems queer," she said, "to be able to sleep at what hours we will, and to eat in the same way."

She looked round as she spoke. More quickly even than Wyndham had done, she recognized the contour of Etna against the sky. "It seems, she said, "that we have come to the right place. We have won the first bout, if no more. But where is the mist? At this time of year, I had heard that you can't see ten yards, even at noon."

"I suppose the tempest swept it away."

"So you said it would. You were right about that. I wonder what the orchards look like. Isn't it true that the oranges grow in the misty months, and when the sun comes they are soon ready to pick?"

"Yes. So I was told. An orchard must be a strange sight. It is hard to imagine thousands of trees with growing fruit on them in no order at all. I believe all the millenniums of cultivation haven't succeeded in making it grow in regular rows, or equally on all branches, as you would think that it would. Of course, the leaves in the hothouses were in the same mess."

"Well, we can see them when we have fed. They can't be very far from here. And it's too early in the season for the automata to be coming picking the fruit, even if they will still go on doing it from now on."

"We mustn't go far from here. We shall have to leave everything that we can't carry about; and I thought we could use this as a house. It's a safer one than we should be able to make for ourselves, and, if we don't start it again, it will stay here for ever."

She considered this with a doubtful frown. "We should have to promise each other that we'd come in and out at the same time. I don't mind, if we do that."

He thought her reception of his idea cold, and her condition fantastic. "I don't see," he replied, "why we need trouble about that. It can't move, if we don't start it again. Why worry as though we thought it might?"

"Well, I should. And suppose it *did*? It might carry one of us away where we should never get back or, if we did, after years, we should and the other had wandered off, looking for us."

Put thus, it was not a pleasant idea, and so, seeing the gravity of her eyes, he assented to a proposal which, in any event, might not have been far from what would have occurred; for neither of them was likely to go far from the other's sight, being alone together as they were, and she under a menace which, as they could not tell what it was, must still walk beside them, a constant, indestructible fear.

After that, being in full accord, and with a pleasant sense of exhilaration at the novelty of the coming days vanquishing colder fears, they ate together—an anarchistic novelty in itself—and decided to leave the plane and set out to explore the land which was to be theirs in the coming years.

What was there to fear, though they should leave all their possessions in the plane, and be away till the twilight came? They had not been used to entertain the dreads, or to take the precautions, which had been normal in lawless times. The idea of theft, its use or occasion, had left the world. Fears of savage men or wild beasts had been equally obsolete for many generations past. They had been taught to believe that beasts of prey, and most others, had been cleared from the whole face of the earth. Certainly, if any remained, it had become a matter for the automata, not for them. The age when men had sought the wilderness that they might find beasts there, and kill them in dirty, dangerous ways, had been succeeded by saner ideals and cleaner customs. And now, even the harmless fellow-beings among whom they had grown up had elected to leave the world. They were alone on an empty earth.

It was true that some of the automata might still be— indeed, almost certainly were—pursuing their daily tasks, indifferent to the fact that their masters controlled no more. There must be respect for them. There might be need to keep out of their way. But, intricately and inter-dependently though they were made, and much as they could do without immediate direction or supervision, it was yet only in pre-designed repetitional ways. None of them—if there were any here, of which there was no sign—would attack the plane. They would not even know that it would be there.

The sun shone, though the sky was streaked in places with flying cloud. It shone on a peaceful scene, not suggesting fear. They stepped out to feel at once its warmth, and a wind that was chill to them. They had not thought until now of clothes as a protection from cold. The single garment and the flexible sandals they wore had been nothing more than a conventional mode, part of the negative reticence to which existence had sunk; but they saw now that there would be more urgent considerations to replace those which had died with yesterday's funeral pyres.

"If we climb, Wyndham said, "to the highest point we can find, we shall see what the land is like, and decide where it will be best to explore. Besides, as the day will grow in heat, we cannot tell how much we shall be going up to a cooler place, and coming down again as the heat declines." He attached great importance to that, interpreting a fact which he had been told without the qualifications which it required.

Vinetta assented willingly. Theorising, perhaps reasoning, less than he, she was alert to circumstance, waiting to learn quickly by the event, willing for him to decide whenever her own instincts were still. And as they climbed easily upward by ancient, half-crumbled paths which had been made before history was, to tame the precipitous hills, their gymnasium-trained bodies making no difficulty of the steep ascent, it seemed that Wyndham's reason might have been good, for they took a side which avoided the northern wind, and yet did not protect them from the heat of the mounting sun. Had they been used to variations of temperature, there would have been little cause for anything less than satisfaction in that. For Sicily, as it had been in the ancient days, it was no more than a sunny noon of the middle spring, but when Wyndham said, "If we find it beyond endurance, we may have to fly to another place," she thought it a sensible word.

As the climb began, they passed barren, broken slopes and craggy hollows which had been luxuriantly fertile in ancient days, but now, having been regarded by the automata as too irregular for cultivation—they having more of flatter, richer land than the satisfaction of their masters' demands required—had been drenched, as had more level stretches of stony ground, with a liquid potent to destroy not only plant, but all insect or other life that the soil contained. Now it lay barren and brown to the scorching sun. No errant seeds could be blown from it by any wind to the detriment of the vineyards and orange and citron groves that flourished in the inland valleys

Yet, as they rose, they observed numerous signs that, in these places of permitted cultivation at least, the suppression of promiscuous life had not been as absolute as they had been taught to believe. They came to a jutting angle of rock where they could not only look out to a width of sea, with the opposite Italian coast receding eastward beyond their sight, but down on a land-locked cove with a strip of white-shining sand, where a colony of herring-gulls screamed and flew, looking from above as though they flew low, skimming the sea.

More portentous, and more alarming to those to whom it was so unaccustomed a sight, a golden eagle, with a stretch of wings that seemed enormous to those who looked up, passed over their heads, and then came again, lower, nearer, having no appearance of fearing men, but rather as considering whether they were fit to be meat to him, or perhaps warning them to climb no nearer to where he made his dwelling above the clouds.

At the third swoop he came so near that Wyndham struck at him with the sword that was already bare in his hand. He thought to hack at a wing which aimed a buffet at him, but the great bird shunned the blow with an ease of rapid motion which showed how delusive was the seeming laziness of these slow-beating pinions.

After that, he kept at a greater distance, and after a time, when they turned to another path, lost interest in them, and disappeared over the mountain-top.

The gulls might thrive on that which the sea gave, until, if ever, the posthumous devisings of Pilwin-C6P should take it away, but on what could the eagles feed? It was a question which might have been more puzzling to those with more knowledge of the habits of such birds than either Wyndham or Vinetta had, but it was answered in the next hour.

Climbing higher, they came to grassy hollows among the rocks which the automata had not reached to destroy. Under the temperate mist which had covered the whole Mediterranean basin during the last six months, above which the sun had moved like a dim, white shield, the grass had grown to a vivid green such as that land had seldom known in its natural climatic conditions. Crocus and asphodel flowered, which might have descended from those which bent to Ulysses's feet.

They looked round and down on as fair a scene as the earth can show, with many mountains behind, and beneath the intense blue sea, and on the right Etna's long, snow-sided, serrated edge, with its plume of smoke that trailed away on the wind. They looked with eyes from which the influence of the deadening drug which had wrecked their race had been cleared away, aware once more of beauty and sorrow, of joy and pain, and of the wisdom of God when he paused on the seventh day to observe that the earth was good.

Going upward still, they came to a cave that had been there perhaps for ten thousand years, during which it had more than once been lost and found and opened again, and yet, for all its age, was not the work of nature, but of human hands.

A place of worship of ancient, foolish, forgotten gods: of sacrifices within its sunless chambers, its hollowed altar still little changed, and its cistern still half-filled with a dreadful witness of human bones, of chambers where the priests dwelt, of oracles through which they divined, and of deep store-pits, whether for use of the priests alone or of the tribe they ruled, with steps leading thereto which had, at a dark turning, a fatal gap, through which thief or foe-man would fall into a pit of another kind.

As they stood looking into the mouth of the cave, which twisted so that they could see little of what it was, a thin, wolf-like dog came trotting up, without seeing them at first, moving with the confidence of one who comes to her own home. But as Wyndham turned, she sprang back, with a whining cry. She did not snarl, nor show anger that strangers stood at the mouth of her own lair. She cringed. Her tail drooped. She had an aspect of abject fear.

Yet in a moment her expression had changed.

She paused in her panic flight. She came slowly, tim-idly back. She was at least as strange a creature to them as they were to her, but her first reaction did not suggest that she was ferocious, or inclined to pick a quarrel with these strangers about her gate. Rather she acted as though they were half-forgotten friends, to whom advances should be made with discretion, but still in expectation of being re-ceived in the same spirit.

"It was the automata that it feared," Vinetta said, mak-ing a simple guess; "it must go in a constant dread."

"It is a dog," he suggested, "or a fox, or perhaps a wolf."

"No. A wolf was fierce. It had great teeth. And a fox had a thick tail."

"Well, we will call it a dog. You know how useful they were to men in the old days. We must practice to get them to serve us in the same way."

Vinetta looked doubtful. She drew down fastidious brows. "They used to hang round the feet of man—in their houses. You would not have them living with us?" She was prepared for much, but, crudely considered thus, it was too abrupt a descent from the life she knew.

Wyndham saw he had gone too far, and his own prejudices revolted in the next instant, sympathizing with her own repulsion. "No," he said, "I didn't mean that. But they might be useful in other ways. We shall have time to learn what they are like."

They went on, not entering the cave farther at that time, to which it seemed that the dog had a prior right. They climbed higher yet. Looking back, they saw that the animal followed them, as though in a timid curiosity. Then they saw another dog trotting towards the entrance to the cave. It carried a smaller animal hanging limp in death from its mouth. They saw more of these creatures later, a species of coney that burrowed among these higher rocks, where the automata did not climb. There was an explanation there of how the dogs and the eagles fed, and of why the conies were hard to see.

The dog which was following them barked when she saw her companion, and the second one looked up, but did not reply, having his prey in his mouth. After a moment's hesitation, the first one bounded back to join her mate, and the two disappeared into the cave together.

"They've gone to eat the creature they have caught," Wyndham said. "Or perhaps to give it to young ones they have got inside." It seemed to them a most filthy idea. He added, "Shall we come to that?"

She had a sickening recollection of the steaming entrails of Pilwin-C6P, as they had protruded while he yet lived. The idea of eating such—she put it firmly aside. Why spoil the beauty of land and sky with such thoughts as that? "I don't see why we should."

"No. We will hope not."

A yellow lizard, darting from stone to stone, diverted her mind, though she was not sure that it was a pleasant change. "The whole world," she said, "seems alive."

It was a strange condition to them, to be thus surrounded by fecund, fighting life. "We shall get used to it in
time," he replied. "I suppose they all enjoy it in their own
ways. We have chosen the same. You won't say you are
getting sorry for that?"

No. Of that, at least, she was very sure. Come what
might, she would not regret.

Height piled on height they had climbed, and at last,
when the sun warned them that noon was some hours behind, they came, after hand and foot had been used for a
scrambling climb, to a plateau, narrow and flat, where they
could ascend no more. They were not on any peak of the
Sicilian hill. They were far below the snow level. To the
south and west, Etna still shut out any farther view. But
they had reached a point where they could judge what the
country was, valley and height, and they had gained a wide
view of sea and coast, and the Italian mainland beyond.

They had a view also, broken at times by obtruding
hills, of a wide, concrete road which wound from the
inland groves to where the sea-causeway united what had
once been Messina with Italy. The terrors of Scylla and
Charybdis had been tamed by the engineering skill that
reined the air-currents which had riotously wandered and
ruled the world. The causeway had been lapped for two
hundred years by the quiet waves of a tideless sea. But
now, far, off though they were, they could see the line of
breakers, whiter than it, which beat on its northern side.
What they had been in yesterday's rushing tempest could
be vaguely guessed from what they now were beneath the
force of a falling wind. Compared with the causeway, the
long road seemed a duller white, the reason for which
could only be read at a nearer view.

CHAPTER TWENTY-SEVEN

As they returned, and had no longer the doubt of what was ahead, or to choose a way, they talked, during the easier descents, of the life which they might hope to build in so fair a land, if only the threat to Vinetta, which was in their minds, not on their tongues, should have glanced aside.

Wyndham spoke with some appreciation of the assistance which he had had from the librarian and museum curator—particularly Colpeck-4GZ—but he had found the historian's knowledge of less certain avail.

Avanah had not lacked willingness, and his learning, even concerning most ancient times, had been very great. Some things which he had told of simple primitive methods of existence had been illuminating, and might prove to be of practical value, but in response to Wyndham's natural curiosity, as it had been directed upon his own unrememberable twentieth century, although Avanah had been able to supply much strange, and some repulsive, detail, a credible vision of what the life of that time had been would not emerge.

He tried to imagine them retiring at night into their little, separate houses, where lights blinked or failed amidst patches of unstable darkness, exhausted by a day spent in aimless whirling about, and in ceaseless watchfulness to avoid disastrous collision with other maniacs similarly employed, or, if they should belong to the unfortunate class quaintly labelled "pedestrians," in derision of the fact that they still moved on their own legs, cleansing their sandals as they came in from the stains of the bloody roads.

He imagined them at a later hour in the "kitchens" behind their lairs, baking slabs of raw flesh cut from the beasts they killed. But there would be no consistency even in that. One man might feed on milk, another on fish. There was no settled process in what they did. With filthy hands, often ungloved, they would grope in the dirt which at that time covered so large a part of the earth's surface. Their backs ached, bending to the spade. Diseases of cold and damp caused their limbs to stick out stiffly at grotesque angles. Yet they had some complicated machines. Daily they must read printed words with half-blinded, myopic eyes, to obtain the information which was necessary to enable them to maintain their precarious lives.

No. He could realize separate facts, but a coherent picture refused to come.

Beyond that, what he could understand roused him to a curious repulsion. Primitive existence had its disadvantages, no doubt, as he would soon learn. And so, most surely, had the negative, sheltered civilization which had now faded away. But this period from which his ego derived seemed to have given hospitality to all the horrors of both, and with a bizarre streak of insanity—perhaps *because* of that streak—added thereto.

But of the earlier beginnings of human life he could form pictures, bewildering enough, yet with a greater aspect of reality and a more genial simplicity. He regarded them, however mistaken he may have been, as more primitive, but less barbarous times.

As they repassed the ancient cave, the two dogs came out together, but with no display of hostility. Showing rather a wistful indecision, the one they had first met followed them some distance down the mountain-side, paused, and then came on again, her companion, with greater hesitation, coming some distance behind. Finally he refused to follow farther, and after a moment of whimpering uncertainty she turned, and they raced back together.

Observing a line of descent which appeared easier than that which they had climbed, they bent somewhat to the left of their previous track, and so came upon the great concrete road which they had observed to run from the interior to the sea, and which had appeared to be of a somewhat duller white than the mole by which it was connected with the Italian mainland. Now they saw the cause of this difference. A thin film of volcanic dust had settled upon the life-denying surface, and upon this a grey-green moss, microscopically minute, had commenced to grow.

It had not been a matter which the automata would observe, or which they could report to the superior machines by which they were designed and sent out on their agricultural errands. It illustrated the vanity of attempting suppression of promiscuous life. "I wonder," Wyndham said, "whether it would have saved them if they had had any idea of what fools they were."

He saw that only life can destroy life while the earth's surface remains; it will rise resurgent from any loss, in a new form which will conquer death.

"I expect," Vinetta replied more lightly, "that men always have been fools, more or less. I dare say we're being silly enough now."

"If we are, we know of about five millions who were sillier still," he said, responding to her mood, as it was easy to do. They were finding life to be good in new and almost unbelievable ways. So long as they would remain two, they had no doubt that it would continue so. While that fact endured, they would be bold to face a mutable world. But if either should be alone....

CHAPTER TWENTY-EIGHT

When the next dawn came with little light in a sunless sky, they had cause to be glad of the shelter that the plane gave, and that they had stores of food which rendered them, as yet, independent of what foraging might obtain.

The wind rose again, blowing from a more westerly direction than it had done on the previous day, and bringing torrential rain. The cabin was no longer heated, and though the temperature would not have been regarded as uncomfortably low by those whose bodies had acquired the most moderate adaptability—being, in fact, no more than three or four degrees below that to which they had been accustomed—they found it shiveringly depressing as they waited inactive for the wind and rain to cease.

They exhausted themselves with the practice of such gymnastic exercises as were possible in that narrow space, and when these could be sustained no longer, they searched out additional garments from the stores, finding that these had more than a conventional use.

It was in consequence of this experimental activity that they had their first experience of how easily the foundations of life may shake when there is no precedent of routine to control the eccentricities of human conduct.

Vinetta, finding that the masculine garments, lighter in colour and somewhat different in shape from that which she wore (they being the ones that Wyndham had thought it prudent to bring), did not fall precisely in place above her own, attempted the reversing of one of these, and in so doing cast a loop of cloth briskly behind her neck. She felt it catch, pull, and tear, and turned quickly, but not enough, to find that it had caught upon one of the control levers by which the plane was started upon its lonely journeys.

She looked for one moment of blank consternation upon that small polished bar, not more than five inches in length, which had responded so readily to the trivial pull. She remembered the warning that these levers, having once been set, must not be changed before the completion of any flight which the plane had been directed to undertake.

"Look," she exclaimed, "look what I have done now!"

Wyndham saw, and no words of explanation were needed "What will happen if we put it back now?" she asked. But it was a question to which, unless the dubious experiment should be tried, there could be no reply. Wyndham recalled his experience with the watering automaton, and it did not encourage blind interference now. Doubtless a sufficiently skilled engineer would have been equal to dealing with the emergency, but could they dare to interfere with the intricate mechanism of this automaton of the air, with ignorant and almost certainly blundering hands?

The control had been set for Warsaw, which they supposed vaguely would be in arctic region under the new conditions of weather which were now sweeping over the world. Wyndham said, "If we go north, we shall freeze. Nor do we even know that there will be food when that which we have shall fail."

"You mean we must leave the plane? Within fifteen minutes from now?"

So he did, and to that they agreed, without further words, though consternation was in their eyes.

Already, they could hear rumbling and gurgling movements within the belly of the plane, indicating that its preparations for flight commenced. They could see that it was taking liquid fuel from the great sunk tank which was in close proximity to its landing-ground.

But what of their possessions which were stored in the plane? What of the tempest that raged without? There were no two answers to that. They must save what they could, bundling it out to lie in the drenching storm. They must lose much, for Wyndham's loading had been liberally done. They might be unfit to face the inclemency of the storm, but, one way or other, they must learn to endure unendurable things.

With a haste which put discrimination aside, they began to unload the plane, carrying bundles of tools and weapons, cases of food, utensils and clothing, out into the violence of wind and the soaking rain.

The entrance into the store-room was too narrow for two people, even unburdened, to pass each other, so that they must time themselves to alternate exits rather than to work side by side, as they would have preferred to do, and, as the minutes passed, Vinetta became increasingly apprehensive that the plane would rise while one or the other of them would be inside and the other out, so that she would have ceased the vital salvage at which they toiled rather than risk the possibility of such separation.

"But we are risking nothing," Wyndham said reasonably; "there is nearly ten minutes yet, and we know that these machines are not erratic in what they do."

Perhaps it was natural that his thoughts were more sharply concerned for the securing of that which he had been at care to collect, much of which, at the best, and however irreparable it might be, must be borne away. "We'll manage three more lots, if not four," she heard, as his voice receded.

The next time, as they met, with sodden garments clinging to rain-drenched forms, he burdened to start outward, and she returning with empty arms, he said hurriedly as he passed out, "At the worst, the one who went could fly back."

Her voice followed him, "Then why didn't we go together?"

He had thought of that already. Perhaps it might have been best at first. To have let the plane have its way, and remain within it. To go to Warsaw, and then return by the simple method of setting the controls to Taormina again.

But with half their possessions already spread on the rain-beat ground, it had seemed a more dubious plan. And there was the incalculable risk of whether the plane were equipped for numerous flights without attention they could not give. Suppose that its next flight should have been to some depot of supplies or renovations where it could have renewed itself in essential particulars? Probably not. But they did not know.

Or suppose the weather in the northern skies should be such that it would have no strength to endure?

No. Even together, they would not adventure again into the perilous skies. Into those heights he supposed that man had risen for the last time, at least for ages to come. He had conquered the air, but had been unable to rule himself, so that his curiosity and his cunning had come to this.

But to risk that either should go alone—no, they were alike in declining that. Yet, at the last, Vinetta's anxiety to avoid the risk brought them very near to that which she had been over-careful to avoid.

"You'll make this the last?" she asked, as they met, he passing outward again, and she stretching impatient hands for whatever might be most quickly snatched in that urgent haste.

"I don't know," he said. "We mustn't stop to talk. There are some things that we're bound to have."

He was out of hearing before the sentence was finished. He had thought of some utensils which there might be time to find. There were two minutes yet, if not three. The dashes in and out were very quickly done.

She came out, and would have restrained him, but he pushed past her. "There is time, he said breathlessly. "I shan't run any risk. You can be certain of that. But don't hinder me now."

In an impatient fear, that increased as the seconds passed, she stood waiting beside the door. She had been unconscious of cold as she had toiled, but she shivered now. Her drenched garments flapped in the gusty wind. She did not observe that. The life which had been concentrated upon its physical self was forty-eight hours behind. But she was sick with apprehension and fear. She heard movements within the plane which reminded her of those which had preceded its former flight. In a few seconds, she thought, it would rise. She was right in that.

Wyndham, searching desperately for a package of cooking and frying utensils which the museum had contained, and which he had been assured were essential to the comfort of a primitive existence, had found it, just as he had decided to risk no further second, and just as that premonitory rumble which had alarmed Vinetta had become audible to him also.

He picked up a case which, under other circumstances, he would have unpacked for a double load, and dashed for the entrance passage. In it, he collided with Vinetta, who had decided that he delayed too long, and that her only course of safety was to join him within.

The moment's obstruction was almost fatal.

"It's too late. We'd better stay now," she protested, for one delaying second.

"Nonsense. It's not moving yet. There's time enough but there's none to be wasted."

Wyndham had the advantage of the higher position in the sloping passage, and of the heavy case that burdened his arms. It was of such weight that he knew he could not continue to support it for more than a few seconds longer, and of such size that he had difficulty to avoid wedging it between narrow walls. His resolute advance bore her backward, hustling her, in fact, so roughly that she failed to turn, as she should have done, at the outer door. There were two steps thrust out from this, and below them a drop of about eighteen inches to the ground. Descending in awkward haste, she slipped upon sodden soil.

Wyndham, close behind her, would have thrown out the heavy case, and followed it down the steps. There would have been time for that, before the plane had commenced to move, but that it would have fallen crushingly upon Vinetta as she was regaining her feet.

Obviously, even in that emergency, he could not hurl upon her a crushing weight, nor could he balance himself with that burden to descend the steps. As she rose, he felt the plane move. It was its motion rather than hers which enabled him to loose the heavy case, which fell forward on to the steps, and rebounded to the ground, already six feet below, where it broke with a clattering distribution of quaint articles of several obsolete metals, aluminium, iron, and tin, on the rain-soaked earth.

The next moment, Wyndham leaped. He landed on feet which slipped from beneath him, and rose limping on a sprained ankle, which would be more painful in the next hour.

Vinetta ran to him. "You are not hurt?" she exclaimed, seeing him rise. "Oh, I am so glad!"

She was met by a gust of anger, born of the pain he felt, and the moment of acute fear through which he had passed. "If," he said, "you will not learn to do what you are told, you will wreck us both. It is no thanks to you that I am not up there now, or hurt worse than I am."

Her eyes followed the plane, which had already soared to a great height, seeking a field of flight which no mountains would obstruct, and was lost to sight, as she gazed, in the driving clouds. She was too glad that he was not there, and too conscious of her own fault, to reply with equal heat.

"If you want to hit me," she said, "I don't mind. You are quite right as to what I deserve." The answer amazed him by its accurate reading of his own mind, which it revealed to himself more clearly than he had understood before. Yes, he had felt that to strike her would bring relief. It had been no more than a moment's impulse, but it had been there. Was the path of descent to primitive roughness of conduct as swift as this? And it so, what might he not be doing in a month—in a year—from now?

Certainly, Colpeck-4XP would have been surprised at the acts and speech of the body which his ego had ruled no more than a few days before. Wyndham Smith's surprise—he having the same experiences, the same traditions, the same body with which to deal—was but little less. But the Colpeck-4XP of a week before had never passed through a moment of such anxiety had never felt such pain as Wyndham was feeling now. Yet, however deeply anger had stirred his mind, Vinetta's quieter answer enabled him to recover self-control, and with it he was aware of some measure of shame. "It was my fault," he replied generously; "I stayed almost too long." He regained complacency with the thought; that he had not failed. Pots, frying-pan, and other utensils of even vaguer purpose might be bruised in their abrupt descent, but would still be fit to remind them for years to come of the fact that he had succeeded in what he sought.

"Anyway, I got them," he said.

"Yes," she replied, "you don't often fail."

There was accord between them once more; and they had need of that, and of all the fortitude that they possessed, in the next hours. They stood soaked and cold beneath drenching rain amid the litter of food, clothes, and utensils which were all they had been able to save from the wreck of the world they knew. They were without shelter, and Wyndham walked already with a limp which was to become worse.

"We've got to do something," he said, "we can't stand here. We should die of cold."

"We should be warmer if we were walking about."

"I don't know how much I could. There's something wrong with my leg."

"There's the cave where the wolves are."

"They're not wolves; they're dogs."

Vinetta observed the irritation in his voice. Neither of them had yet experienced the moral degenerations that results easily from discomfort or pain. But she had sense to see that it was not a time for disputing on such questions as that.

"We'll call them elephants, if you like," she replied equably. "It's a long way off. But it looked like a good cave. And it's the only one we know."

"How will the beasts take it?"

"They seemed friendly enough. Anyway, we ought to be able to deal with them."

"We should be a long while getting everything up there."

"We shouldn't want everything at once and we've got all the time there is."

Wyndham hesitated. His ankle was throbbing in an unpleasant manner, even though he leaned his weight on the other leg. It had taken hours, in better weather, to get up there. But he saw the proposal to be, in itself, not merely sound, but attractive. It had appeared to be a most desirable cave, and he saw a home—a lair which would be their own, and where there would be a sure meeting-place if they should wander apart—to be their most urgent need.

He was reluctant to plead his own infirmity as an obstacle, and he was utterly ignorant of the nature of sprains, or the effect which prolonged exertion would have.

Falling into the same scale, there was a strong reluctance to start out on a vaguer search: to limp about in the rain for a rest they might never find.

"Anyway," he replied, as though the proposal had been already agreed, "it's no use standing here. The sooner we start the better."

"We must take some food," she said, "but not much. Not till we know that we're going to settle there. We should feel silly having to drag things back."

She looked at the way he moved, in a frowning doubt. It was no more than a slight limp, but there was a wide difference from yesterday's easy stride. And it was her fault!

There was no doubt about that. She added, "I'll carry any-thing that we must. You'll need to have that sword free, if the elephants want to argue it out."

He did not agree without protest, but she had her way in the end. He walked on as erect and free as his limp al-lowed, and she went beside with a burdened back. If the spirit of Munzo-D7D could behold them now, he might reflect that the punishment of their insurgence had been speedy to come. Avanah-F3B would have regarded them with different and more curious eyes. They had taught in their periodical schools, which were empty forever now, that all forces hostile to man, both animate, and inanimate had been exterminated or tamed; but here, in two days' time, their boasted civilization had gone like a faded dream, and there was the sword at the man's side, and the load on the woman's back.

CHAPTER TWENTY-NINE

As they climbed, the skies cleared. They looked up to sunshine and windy clouds. Their clothes steamed in the pleasant heat of the sun.

"To think," Vinetta said, "that we have become glad of such weather as this!"

It was a lesson they were re-learning at every hour. That which before had brought no discomfort had brought no joy. The weather had been the same from childhood to death, and they had regarded its controlled perfection with an indifference which did not change. So it had been in every experience of life. Men had resolved that pain should be expelled from the world. They had had their way, and pleasure and pain had gone off together. Were men wrong to make war on sorrow and pain? That would be hard to believe. Yet was it not a fight which they must wage, but, at their peril, they must not win?

Wyndham did not vex his mind with such questions as this. Pain had become a neighbour too close for his peace, and when men speak of its salutary nature it is usually farther away. He rested at times, but found little relief from that. His ankle had become hot and swollen, and it seemed to him that each time he rose it had become worse during those times.

"What shall we do," he said, "if it become worse? If my leg go bad? I must have broken something inside."

Their eyes met in troubled ignorance, from which came a greater fear than they would otherwise have had.

Vinetta would have him stop more than once, but, as the pain became worse, so did the instinctive desire to have some sheltered place he could call his own, in which he could lie secure, either to recover or die.

Once, while they sat by the side of the path, on rocks which were already hot and dried by the midday sun, they were soaked again by a sudden shower which, within five minutes, had passed away. Vinetta took little notice of that, having a greater trouble now, which she saw to have arisen from her fault; but Wyndham found actual comfort, his hot ankle feeling the relief of the cooling rain.

"If the rain had not stopped," he said, "it would have got well. It is that it needs."

Vinetta took what hope she could from this sanguine view. She looked up for clouds. But the wind came from the west, and in that quarter the sky was clear.

When they were some distance below the cave, they paused at a wayside spring. Vinetta looked at many footmarks in half-dried mud. "This," she said, "is where the elephants drink."

Very gladly they did the same, finding more pleasure in that than they could have supposed that drinking could ever give, for the afternoon had become very hot for those who climbed in the sun.

Vinetta said, "If you will stay here, I will go on, and see whether there will be any trouble with the—dogs."

"I can't let you go alone. If there's fighting, it's my place to do that."

"I wasn't thinking of that. I want to make friends if I can."

"And if they don't look friendly, you will come back without going close?"

"Yes, of course. I don't want to get hurt. I want you to rest, if you can."

Reluctantly he gave way. He was so lame now that every upward step was torture, and he was in no condition to enter into an argument of force with two active animals whose methods of warfare were unfamiliar.

There was, to him, an even stronger inducement in that running spring, into which he had already plunged the throbbing foot, finding in its coolness, if not healing, a quick relief.

Vinetta went on alone. She went with the feeling that she had taken a delicate mission, but without thought of using force or fear of attack. She blamed herself, with some reason, for the misadventures of the day. It was her carelessness that had started the plane. Her impatient fear that had obstructed Wyndham when he would have descended safely had she trusted him. She saw that it had become her part to retrieve the position as best she could.

She came close to the cave without meeting either of the dogs, which was not how she would have preferred it to be. She judged soundly that to enter in their absence was not the road to a friendly understanding. But, when she was no more than ten yards away, the female dog came out, not as being aware of her presence, but as having other affairs on hand.

She bounded two or three yards up the rocky face of the hill, ignoring the path, and then stopped abruptly as she became aware of Vinetta's presence. Then her hairs bristled, and she uttered a low ominous growl.

Vinetta had sense enough to stand still, and to speak in a friendly tone. Her voice had an instant effect. Bristles sank, and the growl changed to an uncertain bark.

Had Vinetta shown either anger or fear, it is likely that she would have had the fangs of a powerful animal at her throat. But she remembered the experience of the previous day. She thought that patience would win if only the other dog did not appear too soon.

She was fortunate in this, and in the correctness of the judgment which she had formed.

The animal, doubtless descended from ancestors which had been the friends and servants of men, proved to be of a timid friendliness, only anxious to know that she would be met in the same spirit. They were almost equally strange to one another, but there was nothing in the experiences of either to rouse distrust. The dogs had their own reason for fear, but their enemies had not a human smell.

Tentative advances from either side came to close contact at last. Vinetta endured a cold nose on her naked leg. She stroked, for the first time in her life, the hair of a living quadruped. They entered the cave together, for Vinetta to be nervously introduced to three two-month-old puppies. Their occupation was repugnant to her, being the playful worrying of the fleshless remnant of a coney, on a floor that was not free either from bones or dung. But she saw that the cave was spacious, and with a plurality of chambers, some of them being lighted by high slits in the rock. It might be a better home than she had expected to find, and, if they could dwell together in peace, there would be room both for the dogs and them.

But exploration could wait. Her present doubt was whether the absent dog would be as friendly as his mate had proved. Should she go back now, or wait to be introduced to him as an accepted guest in his own lair? With some doubt, and perhaps more courage than wisdom, she resolved to remain, and was justified by the event. The dog came in with a coney in his mouth, which it seemed to be his habit to provide for the family larder. After an uncertain moment he accepted the position, making no friendly advances, but confining himself to a watchful neutrality. Vinetta decided that the time had come to return to Wyndham, who had found her absence too long for his own peace, though he had had sufficient discretion to await her at the spot where they had parted.

CHAPTER THIRTY

The dogs were together, and watched with a silent intentness, but made no hostile demonstration, as Wyndham, with some support from Vinetta's arm, limped into the cave.

He was anxious to rest, but went on to an interior chamber, separate from that which the dogs occupied. There was satisfaction in the spaciousness of this rock-hewn dwelling of prehistoric man, which offered a better home than they had thought, or could reasonably have expected to find, or to make with their own hands.

But there was no place for rest better than the stone floor on which they sat, finding it dry but hard. It offered little comfort for the hours of darkness and sleep. No men, of any period or condition, would have viewed it with complacency in that particular, and to these two, who were only beginning to experience the annoyance of physical discomfort, it was impossible as a place of rest.

"I must go down again," Vinetta said, when they had eaten a meal together. "I can bring a bundle of clothes on which to lie, if nothing better than that."

"They will be wet now."

"They will have dried in the sun."

"I don't want you to go alone."

"What else is there to do?"

Wyndham did not know how to answer that. It was evident that if he should go alone, even if it should be a physical possibility, it would be dark long before he could struggle back. It would be the same if they should go together, and what protection or help could he be to her, lamed as he was?

She added, seeing that her question had reduced him to silence, "The most important thing is that your leg shall get right again. You can see it's the walking that makes it worse."

He could not deny that. He had dread, for her sake as much as his own, that it might get worse in some way that would cause his death. Or if he should be crippled, it would be poor prospect enough. Reluctantly he gave way, and she set out alone, looking back as she went out with a glance of courage and love that haunted him during the long hours of her absence, as though it were the last he would ever see.

His thoughts were sombre enough for this while. In the stress of accidents and misadventures which the day had brought, Vinetta appeared to have put the fear of Pilwin's threat out of her mind, but it was easy to recall it now, and to remember that Munzo and he had had the resource of the whole earth under their control. Was it likely, with so much at stake, and with such power in their hands, they would have deceived themselves with a plan so futile that it would never even reveal itself to those whom they had so contemptuously warned? It was beyond reasonable hope.

Even without that, might it not be thought that Pilwin's confident prediction that his life would endure for ten days, or more probably less, was already being fulfilled? Surrounded by circumstances that they were unfit to face and inexperienced to control, were they not already blundering rapidly down their deathward way?

He was in this mood when the female dog trod silently into the chamber, now darkening to a deeper gloom than the outer twilight, and came curiously towards, him. He felt a wet nose on his shin, and then a long, red tongue shot out, licking diligently the inflamed ankle. Wyndham had a moment of doubt as to the purpose of the active tongue. Did the animal confuse that injured leg with the flesh of the dead coney which the puppies worried in the outer cave? In a more combative mood he might not have allowed himself the second's pause which showed the harmless nature of what she did.

As it was, he took an unreasonable satisfaction from the contact of the licking tongue. "That," he thought, "is the way in which they heal themselves, when they are damaged in the rough life they live. I will suppose she has healed me now." Vinetta, entering with a burdened back in the deepening gloom, saw the animal lying close to Wyndham while his hand caressed a rough head, as no man had done for three centuries past—in fact, since the passing of the decree by which dogs and other domestic animals had been condemned to extermination, as being unsuitable for a highly civilized and mechanised world.

"She has healed my leg," he said, "in a way that these creatures know."

Wyndham said the next day that his ankle was much better, imagination and courage assisting diagnosis of that which as not really a bad sprain. To support this assertion, he hobbled about. Better it might be. She would not dispute that which they both wished to believe, but it was evident that it was not well.

Clearly, they must be parted again, with whatever reluctance it might be faced. They had no fear of the dogs now. Rather she thought of them as likely to give warning of hostile approach, or even protection, to a wounded man.

The danger, vague, imponderable, but no less formidable menace for that, was on Vinetta, and appeared to them a darker cloud as more immediate troubles became less. But they would be without means of life almost at once, if they should both remain in the caves. Even water must be fetched from the spring. And there were many things, priceless to them, which were now scattered at the mercy of sun and rain, and of the gulls, which had risen, a screaming crowd, when Vinetta had returned last night to the scene of that rushed and scrambled salvage beneath the rain.

She went alone, as she must, putting a brave front on her fear, and coaxing the two dogs to be her companions, to which they consented gladly at first, but withdrew at about the same place, and in the same order as before, when they had found that she was resolved on a downward path. Returning with a can of the water they needed, she set out again, to be joined and then abandoned in the same way.

It was clear that the dogs had a dread of descending to the lower levels which was shared by smaller creatures. For, from when the cave was a few minutes' walk behind, she saw no lizards upon the path, no conies scuttling among the rocks.

So the next week went. Vinetta experienced the indignities of toil and of hardening hands, for there was much to salve, and the burdened upward journeys were long and hard.

The dogs persisted in their refusal to follow her even to the lower hills, except on one occasion, when the female appeared to forget her terror for a time, until, at a sudden memory, or more probable scent, she stopped dead, stood for one shivering second as though paralysed by fear, and then rushed back, whining, and with her tail abjectly between her legs.

Vinetta stood for some moments after this, in doubt whether she should continue downward. Was the animal's instinctive terror a warning which, if it were heeded, might save the life of one whose senses were more obtuse.

So it might be. But the scene continued peaceful and quiet. She reflected that she might never find courage to venture down again, if she should turn back now from a shadow she could not see. She bared Wyndham's sword, which he had insisted on her wearing when she was out alone, and went on with a resolute front, and a shaking heart.

Nothing happened at all. Talking it over at night, they agreed that the shadow of fear was upon all the creatures who had escaped the general massacre which the automata had perpetrated over so large a part of the earth's surface. It was a shadow, they supposed, that would slowly lift. Yard by yard life would spread down the hillsides again. New generations would be born in whom there would be less and less of the inbred fear. The gospel of regnant death had destroyed itself, and the better gospel of life would resume obedience to the divine command.

But if Vinetta had fear in the daylight hours, and must toil when muscles were tired, and become familiar with the degradation of dirt, and if Wyndham must spend long hours of fretful anxiety as to whether she would return, and of anger at his own incapacity, yet there were compensations for both, beyond the experience or imagination of anyone of the five millions who had preceded them on the deathward path which all men in turn must tread.

To Vinetta there was the twice-daily pleasure of her loaded return; the reunions which had a poignancy only possible to two who are alone in an empty world; the sharp hunger which gave a pleasure to the taking of food—as the tired muscles found pleasure in rest—beyond anything which she had conceived as possible in the painless life which was now so utterly, so unregretfully, gone. And after that there was the satisfaction of security in the sheltered cave behind the lair of the watchful dogs, and the joy of comradeship.

To Wyndham also there was a sufficient, though somewhat different, pleasure in sorting and cleaning the articles of a permanent nature which Vinetta brought, and in arranging or storing them away in the recesses of the man-made caves. It gave to both of them a joy of possession, of wealth, which also had been outside the experiences of their previous lives. He had by this time thoroughly explored the caves, and knew the extent and potential strength of this dwelling of ancient priests. It was in the course of that exploration that he came nearly to a worse accident than that which had lamed him already. Indeed, it may be said that the earlier fall saved him from what would have been the more serious injury.

There was a hole in the inner wall through which he could look down into a further chamber, a round pit, having a depth of fifteen or twenty feet, such as might have been used in ancient days for the storage of treasure, or perhaps grain. There was no approach through that hole, but farther to the right there was a winding stair. The stone steps, steeply cut, twisted spirally to the left, the light falling upon the right-hand wall, and in such a way that the steps were partly in darkness.

Wyndham descended five of these, very slowly, their steepness being difficult to one who had a stiff and painful ankle on which he was reluctant to throw his weight. To that slowness, and a warning whimper from one of the dogs, who had been watching him in an obvious disquiet, he owed his life, or the chance of a broken limb which, in that place, might have been the same thing.

For the sixth and seventh steps had been most cunningly cut away, not entirely, but so that there was no more remaining than about nine inches from the wall, and on these fragments there fell a light, which was faint, but sufficient to give assurance and guidance to steps which were not there. Wyndham, stretching out a tentative foot, saved himself; but with great difficulty, even so, where there was nothing at which to clutch.

Waiting till his eyes became more used to the gloom, he saw a pit beneath him, narrow and very deep, from which, had he fallen, it would have been very difficult to escape, even had his limbs remained whole, which would have been improbable after such a drop.

He saw that they who hollowed out these store-chambers from solid rock had had a thought of thieves, and had prepared for them a dreadful trap. But for those who knew, there was sufficient width of step on which they could tread, perhaps with the aid of a friend's hand above or below.

For himself, lamed as he was, he resolved that the store-pits should remain unused, at least to a further day.

CHAPTER THIRTY-ONE

On the eighth day Wyndham, who had relieved Vinetta by fetching water on the previous afternoon, resolved that he would be equal to making the journey with her. There was still much to bring up, for what two people can throw out in fifteen minutes may be much more than one can carry in fifteen journeys up a mountainside. He silenced Vinetta's protest that it would be too great an exertion for a leg that was still of doubtful soundness, with the easy promise that if he found the first journey hard, she should go the second alone.

The wild storms of the first day had been succeeded by light northerly winds and clear skies. The nights were still chilly, but the days were cloudless and very warm.

The shadow of Pilwin's threat had become less menacing, more remote, as the days had passed without any sinister incident, and it became an increasingly reasonable conclusion that the danger had been successfully avoided by the speed with which they had taken to the air, or that they had foiled it by changing the direction in which they flew. They even discussed the probability of Pilwin having spoken a baseless threat, in a final effort to persuade Vinetta to the end which he saw her otherwise likely to miss. That might be no more than a poor guess, but they felt that, whatever the explanation might be, the shadow of death withdrew.

So it was in pleasant accord with themselves and the earth which had become so entirely theirs that they went down the track which was now well-marked, even as it descended the higher cliffs. They caught inland glimpses of vineyards and citron-groves, and agreed that the exploration of what must soon be a main source of food-supply as their stores declined should not be long deferred, even for the urgency of their immediate project.

"In the normal course," Wyndham remarked, "the automata would, I suppose, have been here before now, as the winter mists had been clearing away. So I thought it would be for this year, but Pilwin told me that it was most difficult, even for him, with all his engineering knowledge, to forecast exactly what would occur. Much of the minor machinery will, I understood be likely to go out of action almost at once; but some of it may continue to operate even for years, if the condition of its work be unaffected by other defaults or by climatic changes. In the end there is no doubt that it must go mad, and wreck itself, or just stop and stand about in an imbecile attitude till it rots to dust."

He spoke as one who regards a matter of natural interest which is outside his own immediate concern, but Vinetta answered in a less impersonal tone, "I hope, while I live, I may never see one again. It was through them that the ruin came. Machines and mankind cannot dwell together. They must destroy us, or we them, which we lacked the courage to do."

Wyndham understood how she felt, but considered it in a cooler and more logical mind. "Would you say the same of every tool that we have?"

"They are worked by the power of our own hands."

"But men used other creatures to bear them about, and to draw their ploughs, in most ancient days."

"They were creatures of living blood."

"Men also used the powers of water and wind."

"They were forces already here. They did not bore into the entrails of earth, establishing dead power to replace that of life."

Wyndham did not deny that. He wondered whether men might not have made machinery to obey their wills, and still taken a fairer road to a nobler end. But he could see no certain answer.

What they had done was plain enough, and had come to a most absolute end, unless they two could re-people an emptied world.

"Well," he concluded, "I will say with you, I do not want to see them again. We will look for a greener earth."

"It is of no use saying that. They are coming now."

Her voice had become sharp with fear. Wyndham followed her eyes, and saw that her words were true.

They had come to the point where, as they rounded the mountain-side, they could see far down, far of, in the clear air, the whole line of the causeway that crossed the narrow Messina Straits. On it black dots moved. Vinetta gazed at them and the blood left her cheeks.

"So they may be," Wyndham allowed. "But I cannot see certainly. They are too far off."

"But I can. I can see just what they are."

As she said this there was relief in her voice, and her face resumed its natural colour.

"I knew," Wyndham said, "that I allowed that you had wonderful sight, but to see what are there!"

Vinetta's sight had always been a cause of wonder among companions whose powers of vision were normally good, but it seemed impossible that she could distinguish clearly those moving specks. But she had looked with the eyes of fear.

"There are about two hundred of the agriculturists," she said, "and one control, and two killers."

"Killers?" he asked, in so sharp a tone as to show the unspoken dread which had been in both their minds.

"No," she answered, not to what he asked, but what she knew him to mean. "Just the ordinary kind. What they use for insects within the ground."

There was a great relief in her voice, showing the depth of her secret fear. For the first time they spoke freely of that which had been a suppressed dread in the minds of both.

"It wasn't ever," he said, "a reasonable thing to have feared."

"No. I told myself that it wasn't as though there had been any trail to follow. Not when we came through the air. It would have been different at Mount Ida. They may have relied on our going there."

"There wouldn't have been any trail there."

"Not exactly. But they might have used some of my clothes. I've always had a doubt that a robe went from the gymnasium. You can see how that might happen without my being sure. That is why I changed into Swartz-02A's cloak."

Yes. He could see that. But they had not gone to Mount Ida. And there was no menace in the automata which were approaching now. "All the same," he said, "we don't want them here. I've grown to loathe them since I came out of the influence of the drugs that we used to take. I hope someday we shall be able to stop them coming over that mole. That is, if they don't end themselves, as I hope they may."

"You'd need machinery to do that!"

They laughed easily at the paradox of the idea. It had become easy to laugh, with the knowledge that the approaching regiment held no menace to them. But their hatred did not lessen for that.

"A storm," he said, "such as we had last week, would sweep them away, if it come at the right time."

So it might be. But now the skies were clear, and the wind still, as the automata came over that broad causeway, moving two abreast, with the control behind them, and the two killers closing the rear.

They were a weird sight, but less so than might have been witnessed almost anywhere on the earth's surface half a millennium earlier. For as the automata had developed in the range and complexity of their undertakings, there had been a tendency to produce them in the closest possible imitation of men. This had been particularly the case with the domestic automata, of which the more expensive designs had approximated so closely to the human form in appearance and action that it might be unsuspected by a casual guest that the demure parlour-maid who waited upon him was not compact of living flesh.

But as these automata became commonplace (and class after class of the community had been urged to cease breeding under the threat that their children would starve in a world which would no longer pay wages to chauffeurs, field labourers, or domestic servants who could be so inexpensively replaced), to manufacture them in human likeness became an outmoded fashion. The truly modern woman did not desire that she should be considered sentimental enough to employ a fallible human housemaid, who might be ill at inopportune times, and would not consent to be broken up quietly when the time should come for her to be replaced by a newer specimen.

Only the Major Killers had still been cunningly fashioned in human forms, with the reasonable purpose that the hunted beasts might continue to rear mankind, thinking that they were human hunters on whom their teeth broke in vain, and who were forever upon their tracks.

The two hundred agricultural automata which now advanced over the causeway, moving on caterpillar belts at about six miles an hour, bore a superficial resemblance to the smaller pattern of battle-tank which was designed by the barbarians of Wyndham's own century, the blundering progress of which had often been more fatal to the occupants of its own entrails than those against whom it fought.

They would operate upon broad, straight, concrete paths, between double rows of the vines or orange trees which it was their duty to tend, reaching out long, flexible arms on either side, which were adapted for stirring the soil, pruning the branches, or gathering the fruit, as they might be directed from the control automaton, shaped like a squat, round pot, which had them in charge, and which was itself controlled by the governing automata at Budapest, that being the central station at which all food-producing activities were organized and directed.

The two killers were of a different appearance. In form they resembled rather elongated black swine, having six legs, and a flexible proboscis which they could project to a length of two or three feet or withdraw until it was no more than the upper lip of a strong-toothed snout, with which they would crunch their prey. They had a capacity for scenting living flesh, in all except human form, which was so keen that it would follow the smallest worm or insect beneath the ground, pushing after it until its flight—if it had been alarmed—ended in inevitable capture. Their normal duty was to follow the work of the agriculturists on the cultivated levels, but they might at any time be drawn aside if they should encounter the scent of a quadruped, the keenness and pertinacity of their pursuit being in proportion to the strength of the scent, which was itself regulated by the size of the animal upon whose traces they came.

As the cultivated lands had become increasingly barren of anything on which they could feed, they had been more easily drawn aside, and become more persistent in following any creature of the higher rocks of whose existence they might become aware, so that the terror of the dogs lest they might leave a scent which would bring these creatures upon their trails, in pursuits which would never tire till they were exhausted and caught, is easy to understand.

Having learned what they were, Wyndham and Vinetta went on, with the same assurance that they were too far off for them to see anything more of them for that day, and with the confidence that they would meet with no interference if they should keep out of the way of the invaders, as it should be easy to do.

"After all," Wyndham said, "they will be working for us, cultivating the fruit on which we must learn to live when our stores of better food are consumed."

"But we must not let them gather the fruit and send it away."

"No. We can be before them in that."

"What will they be likely to do when they find that the fruit is gone?"

"I suppose, nothing at all. It would be as though the crop had failed. But, in fact, the question will not arise. The quantity we shall need, or have time to pick, will make no difference to them. And they can do what they will with the rest. They can collect it for the manufacture of food for men who are all dead. It will be nothing to us."

Vinetta's mind had wandered to consider what he had said about living mainly on fruit, which sounded to her like too much of a good thing, if no worse than that.

"The dogs," she said doubtfully, "eat the conies. I wonder what they would be like if we get tired of the grapes."

"They have a filthy taste," Wyndham assured her. "I gnawed a strip of flesh which the puppies tore, while I was confined to the cave. It made me sick. You would not like it at all."

"It seems to suit the dogs."

"We should not like killing them."

"But the dogs would do that for us. They will do anything they can. They like praise."

"Well, so they would. We might try burning the flesh. We know that is what the barbarians did. I have that burning glass from the museum which will make a fire on a sunny day. We must find something to burn."

"So we could. There are still trees on the steeper cliffs."

So they forgot the automata for the time, as they talked of their own concerns.

CHAPTER THIRTY-TWO

It was a few days later that Wyndham went out alone, as he was beginning sometimes to do, to watch more closely the operations of the automata, and to decide how nearly the crops of oranges and citrons which had grown, but not ripened, in the warm mist of the winter months, would be fit to pick. The problems of how, or whether, they could be stored, or how far they might continue to mature as the seasons changed, had still to be faced.

He went without fear, for he knew that the killers were trained to aversion from human flesh, nor would he have been without hope that his intelligence would be sufficient to foil them, even had they started to hunt him down. He thought rather to observe them at their work, and to consider how, if in any way, they could be safely destroyed. With his new vision of life, he hated these automata whose whole occupation was destruction of the sentient life that they were unable to share. He was even repelled by the coney-killing habits of the dogs, and more by Vinetta's suggestion that they should learn to live by the same means.

He had a mind more given to abstractions than hers. It was the immediate practical issue at which she looked. They had to live, as she meant they should, and the lives of a thousand conies were of no account by the side of that. Yet his reflections, wandering into abstractions of vaguer shape, must end at the same gate. To destroy life is to create. Destroy death, and life will go out by the same door. Even individual immortality would have the unavoidable result that generations which would have followed would never be. He saw that which baffled; but nothing to excuse the sin by which mankind had ended so much of the rich life of the earth, and so nearly ended itself. There had been deaths from which had risen no further life. Deaths abortive, blaspheming the creation of God, such as those which the killers were dealing now.

Or, at least, which they would have dealt, had the opportunity been theirs. But he saw them smell with their delicate proboscides around tree-trunks where no insects crawled. He saw them burrow into soil which no earthworms lifted, which was stirred only by the stretched arms of the agricultural automata, the metal fingers of which raised and crumbled it round the roots of the grateful trees.

He looked at the hungry, restless killers, wondering how they could be destroyed or disabled, so that whatever remained of sentient life might endure in the emptied soil. He did not think that it would be easy to do.

The covering of their black bodies was a metal alloy which was smooth, supple, and very strong. It was not formed of loose plates or the links of mail. It was a glove-like skin. All was metal, even to the cloven, hog-like hooves. Their mouths, which, when the proboscides were drawn back, showed rows of razor-sharp metal teeth, were to be avoided with care.

Behind them there were apertures from which vapour would issue at times, being from the combustion that went on within. Perhaps some weapon driven in at those openings might cause damage sufficient to end their activities? He considered that they must ultimately depend for their strength upon consumption of the creatures they caught. Getting no more than an occasional insect, their enduring vigour could not be much! Perhaps there might be hope in that.

He would do nothing rashly. It was a matter for careful thought, where error could not be risked. His lifelong inhibition against interfering with the machines made it easy to be cautious now.

But he walked past them, seeing that they took no notice of him, and observed again how hungrily they pursued their hunting, and with what meagre results.

CHAPTER THIRTY-THREE

The killer walked on the edge of the concrete path, which it preferred to the softer soil over which its proboscis hovered restlessly, stretching for a scent that was not there. At the place where Wyndham passed it and its companion, and walked ahead without troubling to give a backward glance, its proboscis swayed restlessly towards the path, and then jerked away. It could scarcely have been more irresolute, more confused, had it been capable of a conscious thought.

Very strongly it smelled man, which it had been taught to avoid. Faintly, but unmistakably, it smelled dog. Large dog, which it was fiercely eager to reach. More, in fact, than one dog, for its perceptions were so keen, so delicate, that it could distinguish the two animals that had been rubbed against human legs, and even the puppies that had been fondled by Wyndham's hands.

But for that smell of man it would have been already trotting hard, its six legs moving with clumsy speed on the tempting track. As it was, it moved slowly, uncertainly, as though conscious of wrongdoing, and being drawn forward against its will.

Its comrade, working twenty yards behind on the other side of the path, came to the same spot, and behaved in the same way.

Ten minutes later, though still with slow, uncertain movements, they had left the plantations, and, side by side, were climbing the mountain-side.

So they went on, but at a decreasing pace, with longer pauses, and may have been on the point of abandoning a scent which did not strengthen, and was so repellently blended with that which they were forbidden to follow, when they came to the place where the dog which descended with Vinetta had recognized her danger and fled.

At that, their demeanour changed. Here was scent, separate, strong, and rich. It was confused neither with that of Wyndham nor Vinetta, for the she dog, in her abject flight, had taken her own path. The two killers no longer moved like hounds on a doubtful scent. They galloped up the rocks, steep though they were jostling each other in their eager advance.

Soon they came to a place where they were confused by the very plenitude of that alluring odour. They went slightly separate ways, but it was to the same goal from that moment there could be only one end. The dogs might avoid them by constant flight for a week, even a month, but in the end an implacable, unswerving phase would run down a panting, exhausted, or possibly sleeping prey. There would be a moment of futile writhing in the grip of the cruel jaws, or snapping against smooth, tooth-breaking sides, and the two automata would settle down to tear at a common meal. So, at least, it would have been if the last of mankind had left the earth in the grip of the evils they themselves had bred.

Wyndham was at the cave-mouth when he looked back, and might not have done so then had he not heard one of the dogs cry out in fear with a wail like a beaten child.

It may have been that cry which guided Vinetta's mind to the right track. She had come out of the cave, and saw the automata at the same moment as Wyndham. She said, "They're not after us. It's the dogs."

The two animals, which had moved a few steps right and left, and then stood as though paralysed by a sense of unescapable doom, drew at last in shivering fear behind their human friends, as to the sole hope that remained. It was a plea it would not have been easy to refuse, even had their fear of the killers been greater, or their hate less than it was.

Vinetta looked questioningly at Wyndham, as though seeking a decision from him which she felt unequal to make. She said, "You won't find that sword any good."

"No, but we might this."

He walked to where a great stone stood by the mouth of the cave. He bent to it, using all his strength.

Seeing his intention, and that it did not move, Vinetta gave her aid. The two dogs stood watching intently, their drooping tails having lifted slightly, and began to sway in gratitude for a championship which they already instinctively understood. The automata were scrambling rapidly upward, but still some distance below.

Pulled by four straining arms, the great boulder lifted and rolled over into the centre of the sloping path. Wyndham paused, waiting his time.

"Now," he said, "let it go." Their arms strained again, and the stone bounded down the slope. The dogs barked sharply for joy of that which they could not themselves have tried.

The four who watched saw the boulder leap straight downward upon the advancing automata. It seemed inevitable that one at least must be crushed, or tumbled backward the way it came. And then, when the stone was almost upon them, it bounded upon a rib of projecting rock, and leaped clear over.

Unperturbed, as conscious climbers could not have been, the automata continued their clambering upward way.

Wyndham bent to another stone. It was smaller than the first. But it was more tightly wedged. By the time they had it in position, the nearer of the automata was not more than thirty yards away, and they were advancing fast with the strong scent of the dogs' lair drawing them on. The stone struck the first squarely upon the head, bounced upon it, and turned somewhat sideways as it leaped downward, leaving its victim sprawling upon the slope. They saw that its proboscis was crushed and limp, but beyond that they had not time to regard or care what its injuries might be, for the second automaton came on in blind oblivion of its comrade's fate, and there was no time for poising another stone.

"Back!" Wyndham said. "Back quickly! Into the cave."

"Into the cave?"

"Yes. It's the best chance." Through his mind, as he said it, there passed a doubt. What if he were directing them to nothing better than a cornered death? But it was the plan he had formed against such an emergency in a cooler hour, and his judgment was too settled to change it now.

They ran back into the cave, but not in too blind a haste to catch up the puppies and bear them with them, as they passed through the inner chamber, and felt their way down the steps to that deadly gap, in a gloom which was the greater because they had allowed no time for their eyes to adjust themselves from the bright sunlight without.

Vinetta went first, with a puppy under one arm, and Wyndham's hand reaching to hers.

"You cannot go wrong," he said, "It you press close to the wall. I have seen how the steps are cut."

When she said she was safe, he followed, with the other two puppies.

The dogs, with these examples before, and the fear behind, needed no coaxing to follow.

Very cautiously they descended the remaining steps into the grain-pit, timorous of a second trap, but there was no more occasion to fear.

"Keep the dogs to one side," Wyndham said, as they entered the rounded hollow of the pit. "If the killer gets here, he will follow the scent, and may chase them round so that we can all escape by the way we came. Remember the trick Munzo played upon us."

As he spoke, he turned to re-ascend the steps. Vinetta made a movement to follow.

"No, you don't," he said, in a voice she had only heard from him once before. "You stay here. Do as I say. Will you never learn? You would be in the way. You will do your part if you keep them to one side of the pit."

Protest rose to her lips, and died as she remembered how she had brought everything to the edge of disaster when she had interfered at a moment of crisis before.

He went back up the steps, and was none too soon.

Looking upward to the light, he had a clear view of the killer already commencing to descend the steps. With the strong scent drawing it on, it had the eagerness of a living thing.

Wyndham looked at the gap. Was it wide enough to engulf a creature of such length? Would it blunder blindly into the trap, or would it remain there, waiting, perhaps for months, blocking the only exit while they would starve? It was a possibility he had not previously considered. His mind had concerned itself only with the hope that the pursuer would fall into the pit, and with the danger that it might cross the gap. But now, with the quickness of thought, he saw himself labouring with his bare nails to enlarge the hole in the wall through which he had first looked into the pit—toiling at that impossible task while Vinetta starved and the killer waited above the steps.

There was another risk that it might keep close to the wall, and descend, as they had done, on the narrow fragments of the steps which had been allowed to remain. But he had not regard this as a great risk. The killer's legs were set much farther apart than his own, or those of the dogs. He doubted that it would be possible. Besides, what reason was there for it to hug the wall?

Unfortunately, there was a simple answer for that. It followed the scent of the dogs, and where they had gone close to the wall, its proboscis went the same way. Its left side rubbing the walls, a left foot came down firmly upon the jutting fragment of step. A second later, its right forefoot was pawing the air. The black, supple, hog-like body lurched forward, but did not fall; neither could it easily recover itself. The instinct to draw back may have been lacking. However cunningly these automata may have been constructed, however many contingencies they may have been adapted to deal with, there must always have been some events which would find them lacking, some which they would face as fallibly as a man may do, when an unprecedented problem bewilders his mind.

The reactions of the automaton may have been confused by the fact that its left forefoot was firmly planted, and that it could not move to that side, which the wall forbade, when footing failed on its right.

Wyndham saw it with its right foot and its proboscis feeling the air. The proboscis touched him, and shrank back from the human scent. He struck twice with his sword at the smooth shining head, as it hung over the void. There was no use in that. The blade slipped along a surface so hard and smooth he could expect to do no more than damage his weapon's edge.

He saw that the event was in a critical doubt. The killer might hang suspended there; it might draw back and remain a waiting menace, which was perhaps most of all to be feared; or it might even lurch itself successfully over the gap. Thinking to turn a doubtful scale, he caught hold of that outstretched proboscis, and strove to pull it downward with all his weight.

He succeeded almost too well. The beast-like form shot into the pit so abruptly that for one perilous instant it seemed that he was destined for the same depth. It was the backward push of the descending body rather than his own adroitness which enabled him to retain his place on the lower step.

For a long minute he gazed into the obscure depth. Like a dying beast, the automaton struggled and kicked. But those who built that pit, with its smooth, narrowing walls, had done their work well in their distant day. It might struggle or lie still as it would, but it was there that it must remain while the earth endured.

Wyndham went down to where Vinetta waited beside the dogs. "There is nothing more to fear," he said. "You can come, up when you will."

CHAPTER THIRTY-FOUR

The months passed. The automata worked in the orchard groves, indifferent to the fact that their human masters had ceased to need the food which they were diligent to provide. Every week a train of automatic vans had arrived, and departed after loading themselves with the gathered fruit, which, as Wyndham had been glad to observe, did not ripen in a single crop, but, with the partial exception of the grapes, gradually throughout the year.

The summer had been hot and dry, but at the time when the two hundred gardeners were due to leave there came heavy storms from the northwest.

Wyndham, venturing out alone in a windy interval of the rain when the skies were bright, saw, far off, the great causeway hidden in the white foam of the up-flung waves. He had seen it beaten and submerged more than once before by tempestuous seas, and had wondered, with hope rather than fear, whether it might not be breached and finally swept away. He had explored most of the island, more or less, by this time, mainly with Vinetta.

He regarded it now as a secure home, or rather as one which would become secure if that road to the mainland were swept away. For there was ever a doubt of what might come from the larger spaces beyond. But though it might show marks of the buffetings it received from the angry waves, the great mole endured.

Now he saw the long train of the automata moving over the shoreward road, indifferent to the raging wind, with the round pot-like control in the rear. He wondered, with an increasing interest, what they would do when they came to meet the fury of those sweeping waves.

He watched an event which showed that they had no wisdom implanted in them to meet a condition which had been so long unknown to a tamed world. They went on. Had he been endowed with Vinetta's sight he would have taken back to her a more vivid report than he was able to do.

"I have little doubt," he said, "that they have been swept away. They went blindly on to the mole. I watched till the control tank in the rear of all went into the waves. It kept on for some time, though it was entirely covered as often as not. But it went at last."

"Then," she said, well content, "there is hope that we shall not see them again."

It was a hope that grew in the next week, for there was wreckage upon the shore.

They had come at this time to hate all that reminded them of those empty days before life came to its natural flower. They had many hardships now, many difficulties, many doubts, hope and fear alternating as the dawns and sunsets came, but existence itself had become a joy such as they could never have conceived it to be in the painless days.

They gathered possessions of many kinds. They had a sense of owning the earth. Not knowing what the winter conditions would be, and expecting vaguely something much worse than is the lot of that favoured land, they had made a store of grapes dried in the sun. They knew nothing of the making of wine, so that there was fair hope that its curse would long be kept from the lips of men.

They had gathered a store of fuel against the same fear of winter storms and a freezing air; having already learned the making of fires and roasting conies' flesh. They did this on the altar where human victims had groaned and burned countless centuries earlier.

Vinetta looked at the gathered skins of the conies, stiff and foul as they were, and dreamed of garments against the cold. "It is done," she said, "with the bark of some tree. If only I knew which!"

"There is not much choice here," Wyndham replied. "The only trees are those that have endured on the heights, above the belt of the barren ground; and the fruit trees below."

"Well," she said, "we must try with all."

So they struggled to regain fragments of long forgotten knowledge, blundering on through many failures towards infrequent success. But oh, the joy of the gain achieved, of the discovery made.

And, in all things, the five dogs were their faithful servants and friends, as they had been from the day when they had watched their two enemies destroyed by the powerful protectors that they had found. They were such companions that Vinetta did not feel as much alone when Wyndham left her now as she otherwise must have done. And so the time went on, until the night when Wyndham did not return.

CHAPTER THIRTY-FIVE

Wyndham had said with truth that the world was wide. He was right in that. He had guessed that the plot which Munzo and Pilwin had made against Vinetta's life had largely assumed that it was to Mount Ida that they would go. So it had. He was right again. But he was not right in concluding either that they had depended upon that assumption, or that the alternative was that Vinetta should be pursued blindly throughout the world.

When Munzo's pencil had traced its plans beneath Pilwin's understanding eyes, he had expected that it was to Mount Ida that they would go, and he had provided that Vinetta's end would be speedy there. But he had left nothing to chance. The Major Killers were less numerous than they had been at an earlier day, but he knew that there must still be from half a dozen to twice that number which would be in condition for instant service. He arranged for each of these to have a shred of one of Vinetta's garments inserted into its scenting organ in such a way that it would be a continual irritation, urging it, as its construction required, to suck the blood of the woman whose scent it knew.

The whole number of these were sent to Mount Ida to make Vinetta's destruction sure, but, if she were not there, they would not scatter in search over the wide range of the earth, but go systematically to the various points at which the plane could alight, in the neighbourhood of one of which she would be certain to be. They would travel by roads along which they would be able to pause at regular intervals to refuel themselves, as they were designed to do, and so long as these depots should supply their infrequent needs, and their mechanism remained sound, there could be no change or diminution in the blind, fierce impulse that drove them on.

This plan, ordered by Pilwin with his usual careful efficiency, had worked with no more than a single accident. The Major Killers in working order being less numerous than the stations to which the plane might possibly have been directed, Pilwin had had each of them set so that they would visit a second, if the search of the first should find no victim to satisfy their unconscious chemical thirst. This had resulted, with a humour which lacked the audience it deserved, in two of them meeting, while hurrying in opposite directions, and attacking each other with destructive fury as they perceived a whiff of the scent they sought. But there was no safety for Vinetta in this, though one of those destroyed in this fratricidal strife had made Taormina its goal.

It did no more than delay the event, a second killer, which had spent many weeks in hunting round Lake Garda's shores, coming to the Sicilian mole in the early afternoon of a day that was bright and still. The mole was scarred and battered, and looked unlikely to survive through another year, but it was yet whole. There was no wind-driven weight of sea to sweep over it, and wash the deadly invader off. It trotted on at its invariable pace upon level ground, which was about seven miles an hour. When Wyndham saw it, it was advancing along the shore road, at a point which they had often overlooked, but where, he was glad to think, Vinetta and he had never had occasion to go. Wyndham, in no danger himself, stood for one moment of indecision, resolving what he would do. Should he warn Vinetta? There were two objections to that. He was some miles away from the cave, and there would be extra effort, which might be beyond his strength; and the killer might come on Vinetta's track before he should find it again.

He had long formed a most desperate plan against the danger which was now here. In fact, they had talked it over together, and, in its simpler, original form it had seemed as good as, or better than that which had been fatal to the Minor Killer within the cave.

But that had assumed that a good distance would be maintained as the scent was laid. It had assumed that Vinetta herself—Wyndham not being far off—would be the bait of a cunning trap. Wyndham saw that it must be the endurance of human muscles that would be tested against the killer's mechanical strength in a most equal duel. His human wit against the chemical purpose which drove it on.

"Well," he thought, "she must wait my return, till the dusk at least. There is no help for that. It will be well for her if the dusk do not fall and I have not come." He would save himself if he could and he hoped he might, but he could not call it better than a poor chance. Thinking this, he began to descend the hill, so that he would come to the path upon which the killer advanced.

As he did this he began to tear off his garments, of which he now wore several, feeling the chill of the cooling evenings, which, though they were temperate enough, he faced for the first time. He threw most of them away, but kept the one which Vinetta had worn as she had toiled and sweated beside him, bearing fuel into the cave for their winter store.

He had not thought it necessary to tell her that he had taken this, nor that he wore it when he went out by himself, as he sometimes did in these last days.

He descended till he was near the killer, which took no notice of him. He had not seen one of this pattern before, and he liked its looks even less than he had expected. It had the height and girth of a tall man, and its metal body was supple, and smooth, and bright. It had a man-like face, but that which should have been its nose was a cruel beak. Its eyes shone with an inward light, and had for lashes a kind of antennae, which would warn it of, any obstruction while it was still some yards away. It had hairs of a similar utility on its knees. When it fought, its eyes would close metal lids to a narrow slit. Its lower jaw was very large, with long pointed teeth.

Wyndham saw that his sword might as well have been left behind for any use it would be. He knew that the smooth toughness of the metal in which the killer was sheathed would blunt its edge without its own surface showing a mark of the hardest blow. He cast it from him, and stood holding Vinetta's garment in his hand.

He had no wish to interfere with the killer so long as it continued upon the southward road. It was the way he would have it go. He sought only to save his strength, which could be done by crossing a bluff of the higher ground where the road took a wide outward sweep. Doing this, he went at half the killer's pace, and yet arrived on the road ahead, so that he had leisure to sit on a stone and rest for a short time.

While he did so, he tore a long strip from the garment that Vinetta had worn, and laid it in the midst of the road.

Immediately that he saw the killer appear, he stepped forward to the spot where the rag lay. He laid the remainder of the garment beside it, and then commenced to run away, trailing it along the path.

He looked back, and saw that the killer had stopped and picked up the rag. He ran on again, seeking to lengthen the distance the most he could, so long as he could be sure that he was pursued.

He saw the killer swallow the rag, which was fuel to it, though it would have thrived better on living flesh. It went on its knees, smelling the dust. Then it came on again. At a place where Wyndham had trailed the garment a few paces aside, it made a similar bend.

That was conclusive. It had picked up the scent. Wyndham turned and ran. He was no longer concerned to make sure that he would be followed. He had only to keep ahead. But could he do that? Many miles away, he saw Mount Etna's ridge, snow-white and jagged, with one black column of smoke that rose straight upward to a windless sky. The sun was still high overhead. When the sky reddened to sunset behind that ridge, would there have been an end of the race of men? He ran on.

After a time, he looked back. There was half a mile of bare road in view, but the killer was not in sight.

He continued at a hard run towards the mountain which, as the sun sank in the sky, seemed ever to recede. But yet, as the hours passed, it became higher, more forbidding against the sky. There was hope in that, though also a warning threat.

For the last hour he had feared to look back. He knew that he must have gained some ground at first. But since then he had slackened pace, as feet faltered and muscles ached on an upward way. He did not seek to foil the pursuer by any wile, for it was his object to lead it on, and though he knew that he might save himself by casting the garment aside, he did not consider that, for he knew that, should he fail now, fate might not allow him a second chance.

Should he fail now, the next pursuit might be on Vinetta's track, and it was easy to guess how small her chance of escape would be likely to be—even apart from the final risk, which must be perilously taken, whether by him or her.

He did not have to climb the mountainside by the rough tracks which he must have used in more ancient days, a broad zigzag path having been laid by those who, at one time, had made great use of the mountain's volcanic power. But the ascent was steep and long, and by this time he had looked backward and down, and had seen the pursuer less than a quarter of a mile behind.

That would have been margin enough had he been fresh, but now he was urging reluctant limbs, and panting at every step.

On the height of the black and rugged edge, Wyndham left a path which was crusted with frozen snow. The extremity of his exertions had made him indifferent to the icy temperature. Rather, it had served to brace his exhausted muscles for the final peril which was to come.

For a moment, he faced the sunset light that told him that the summit was won. With the next, he had plunged downward into a deepening gloom that yet shone with a shifting glow. The air was hot to breathe, and dry with volcanic dust. The cold of the windswept summit was left behind, and the temperature rose with each slippery downward step.

Soon, as his eyes adjusted themselves to the sombre gloom, he was aware of a pool of liquid lava, blacking and bubbling below. He breathed with labour, a foul, gaseous vapour choking his lungs. Vinetta's garment, now soiled and ragged, was still trailing behind his steps. He heard the killer descending, now twenty yards in his rear. Its muscles did not ache, its speed was not lessened. If the next minute did not shake it off, he would be a dead man, and there would be and end to the human race.

It was not how he had meant it to be. He had imagined Vinetta and himself together, laying a trail which would have ended below, and going away in safety while the killer was still miles behind. This was different, as imagination and actually are ever likely to be.

The killer was now close behind; the hot liquid lava was close before. Already his feet were scorched on a shaking soil. He threw the garment forward, and leaped aside. After he had gone a few yards, he stood still.

For good or evil, success or failure, the game was played. If he had thrown the garment too far—if the killer should elect to follow him rather than it—then it was lost. He knew that he could never struggle up from that crater-mouth at the pace that the unwearied automaton could command, for his strength was done.

For a moment the issue paused. The killer, as though impossibly aware of its danger, or doubtful of the direction in which to pursue its prey, slackened its steps. It stood still. Then the scent of that fatal garment must have reached it through the fumes of the naphtha'd air. It rushed forward. Its legs plunged in the molten fire. Even as it sank, its claws closed on the soiled rag. Its jaws tore, and swallowed, and tore again. So it sank from sight.

Wyndham became conscious that his feet were slipping. His sandals smoked. Wrenching them free, he turned to struggle up from the hot gloom of that sulphurous pit.

He mounted slowly and with panting gasps, having become aware of how spent he was. But his heart sang.

He did not know that he shivered on the cold summit, where the light or the sunset failed. He had no after-memory of how his stumbling feet descended, crunching the snow, with no better light to aid than the stars could give.

It was wide dawn when he came again to the cave, to be met by the barking dogs, and Vinetta's arms.

In the lonely night, she had learned the meaning of prayer.

ABOUT THE AUTHOR

SYDNEY FOWLER WRIGHT (1874-1965) penned over seventy volumes of science fiction, fantasy, classic mysteries, historical novels, poetry, and non-fiction, many of them being published by the Borgo Press Imprint of Wildside Press.

www.ingramcontent.com/pod-product-compliance
Lightning Source LLC
Chambersburg PA
CBHW031408250626
47155CB00004B/1459